THE FORSAKEN: DESCENT

MARTIN FERGUSON

ALSO BY MARTIN FERGUSON

RELIC HUNTERS:

Eagle of the Empire

Curse of the Sands

War of the Damned

Blood of the Dragon

&

Origins of the Hunters

———

THE FORSAKEN:

Wraith

Descent

Cover by Jacqueline Sweet Design
Editing by Karen Sanders Editing
Formatting by Pink Elephant Designs

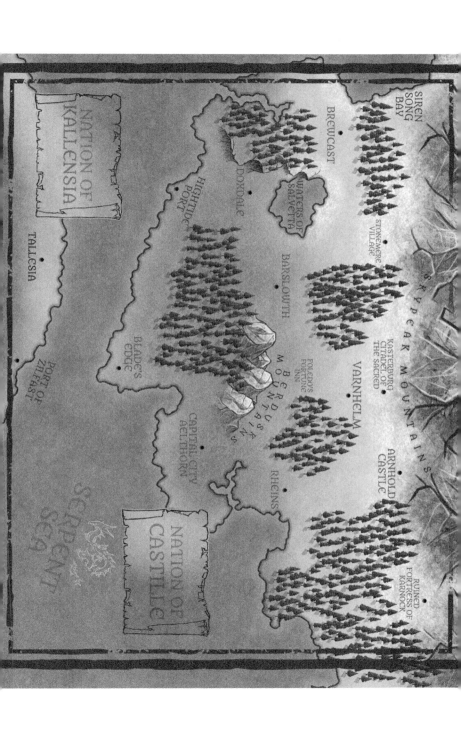

PROLOGUE
THE GUILD

THE CITY OF VARNHELM

In the darkened training hall deep within the keep, a boy of eight years stepped forward upon shaking legs. He stood upon a raised platform, facing a course of narrow wooden beams and boards, held aloft in the air by swinging pendulums. The course ahead was constantly shifting and moving, posing both a challenge of balance, timing, and courage.

'Now!' a voice commanded, and the boy was forced onto the first beam.

He struggled for balance, almost falling as he moved slowly and unsteadily upon the moving beam. Once he reached the end, he waited for the next swinging board to pass. He hurried across as the beams briefly met, stumbling and tripping, barely remaining upright. The boy managed across to the next beam too, and a smile flashed upon his face, proud that he had succeeded so far. His happiness was fleeting as he saw ahead of him blunted spears reach out from the walls to strike any who crossed the swinging beams. Fear and doubt claimed the boy, unmoving upon the board in the face of another obstacle.

'Move!' commanded the voice of his instructor. 'Move or fail!'

The boy, fighting his fears, took a handful of paces, barely missing the first spear before being hit square in the chest by the second. He fell, tumbling from the board and landing hard on the wooden floor below. The impact hurt, the air driven from the boy's lungs and leaving him a wheezing, coughing mess.

'Luthor!' a young girl with dark hair but for a single white streak cried as she hurried to his side. 'Are you hurt?'

'Leave him,' another apprentice, this one a burly, confident boy, called down from atop the obstacles as he traversed them with ease. 'He shouldn't be here if he can't learn this for himself.'

'Shut up, Marek!' the girl yelled back at him.

'He's right,' Luthor moaned as he dragged himself upright on the floor. 'I shouldn't be here! I can't do any of this!'

'Yes, you can,' the girl tried to assure him. 'You just need to try again and again until you've mastered these beams.'

'And what of everything else? Swords, hunting, thieving, alchemy… I can't do any of it.'

'Then I will help you.'

'Girl, back to your lessons,' an unseen but commanding voice called from the shadows. 'And Luthor, back to the course with you.'

'Yes, Guildmaster Brevik,' Luthor muttered as he pulled himself to his feet and took to the beams once again.

———

RUINED FORTRESS OF KARNOCK

With trembling steps, the boy of fifteen years walked the crypt. The light of his aflame torch barely penetrated the darkness of the catacomb, shadows playing tricks with his mind, and the eerie silence fuelling the fear within. His breath came quick as his heart thundered in his chest, his grip tight on the torch and the hilt of his sword. All he wanted was to turn and leave that haunted place as quickly as his legs could carry him, but he had no choice. He had to push on.

'You'd better be right about this, boy,' one of his two companions, a burly and irritable dwarf warned. 'If not, it will be my mace in your skull.'

'Go easy on the lad,' a wretched, gangly man said. 'If it wasn't for him and his links with the Guild, we wouldn't have this contract.'

A sudden movement to his side made the boy recoil and swing his sword and torch, both clattering off a stone tomb and missing their target, a spider that slowly crawled away.

'Easy, lad,' encouraged the man.

'Damn foolish lad,' the dwarf muttered.

'Get a grip of yourself,' the boy told himself, his voice echoing through the catacombs.

He then jumped in fright, almost dropping his aflame torch as a deep, desolate voice called from the darkness in reply.

'Why do you disturb this hallowed ground?'

He looked to his two companions but saw no sign they too had heard the voice.

'I ask again. Why do you disturb this hallowed ground?'

'To... to prove myself,' the boy stammered.

'What'd he say?' grunted the dwarf.

3

The boy waved his torch in all directions to illuminate the crypt, but there was nothing to be seen. The apprentice and the two hired rogues were alone but for the tombs of the dead and the many cobwebs.

'What is your name, boy?' the voice asked.

'L… Luthor.'

The flames of his torch suddenly extinguished, plunging the tomb into darkness.

'What did y…' the dwarf began to say before falling silent.

'Where are…' the man cried out until he too spoke no more.

Luthor turned his head and looked on in horror as he saw his companions, the rogues he had hired for this contract, were pinned against opposing walls. Bone hands reached from the darkness, holding them in place as wounds tore deep of their bodies. Their faces contorted in silent screams as blood tore free of their veins. Gore and organs fell to the crypt floor and flowed as crimson rivers past Luthor and into the darkness ahead.

'You have nothing to fear, my boy. Step forward, Luthor, and prove yourself worthy.'

CHAPTER ONE
SKYPEAK MOUNTAINS

The frost crunched beneath Wraith's boots as she hurried across the mountain road and leapt over a grassy mound, throwing herself to the ground. She waited and listened, hearing hooves upon the road and the squeak of wheels. Unseen, she crawled to the top of the mound and peeked over, watching as a pair of mounted guards escorting a carriage approached. The aflame torch of the Sacred was emblazoned on the armour of the guards and the carriage, the group heading up into the mountains bound for the Kasterburg Citadel.

As they passed where Wraith hid, a young face appeared at the carriage window. A girl of no more than five years of age. Her cheeks were scarlet and eyes red with tears; a potential bound to join the Sacred, as was their command across the realms of Centuros.

As the horsemen and carriage passed, Wraith pondered on their destination, the Citadel of the Sacred. The order of sorcerers and mages was seen as the highest power in the land by many, possible descendants of the Gods who even kings and queens paid homage to. It was demanded that all potentials who showed the smallest glimpse of arcane ability be inducted into the order, whether willing or not.

That could easily have been me, Wraith thought, looking at her hands.

Sixteen years of age, hazel eyes, long black hair but for a streak of white to her left and a deep scar running down a cheek. Beneath her black cloak, furs to keep the cold at bay, and leather and chainmail armour, was a slender and agile form with a hint of muscle. Her shortsword, Shatter, was sheathed at her side, and her cloak contained a variety of weapons and tools to aid her in this hunt, not that it had been difficult so far. The tracks she had been following were clear and easy to trace from the farmlands and shepherds' homes where she had begun this hunt north into the lower reaches of the Skypeak Mountains.

As the carriage and its escort disappeared into the distance, Wraith wondered of Jaks, Jakseyth Sondolar, the mage's formal name. Wraith had only just recovered from their exploits in the cursed village of Stonemere, her first contract for the Guild. Wraith and her allies had rescued Jaks from a cell deep amongst the doom, and in surviving those horrors, an allegiance and possible friendship had been born. Upon her return, Jaks had been promoted from apprentice to acolyte in the Sacred order, and that was the last Wraith had seen of the mage. She wondered what Jaks was doing now and what her new duties as an acolyte entailed.

Wraith surveyed the ground, quickly picking up the tracks that led higher into the Skypeaks. She stopped before taking a single step as, in the distance, a low growl rumbled. Looking down upon her stood a lone brown bear, big and menacing. Wraith's eyes looked into the dark brown of the bear's. She knew the animal could quickly close the gap between them and maul her with claws and bloodstained jaws. The bear continued its gaze, still and silent for a moment.

'I'm not hunting you,' Wraith whispered, as she too remained still, hands lowered, no threat.

The bear growled, roared once more, and then turned away, uninterested.

As the bear lumbered away, Wraith paced on, seeing her breath hang in the air as she climbed upwards. The snow-topped mountains loomed above, and she prayed to the Gods her hunt would not lead her into the frozen tundra. Thankfully, it did not take long for her prayers to be answered as the tracks led her on to a gorge between mountains and then to the entrance of a cave. Chicken, rabbit, and cattle bones littered the ground and led the way into the grotto, where a soft, warm glow invited.

Wraith paused for a moment and waited, gripping the crimson hilt of Shatter and drawing the shortsword, slowly and carefully, revealing the faint outline of an arrow upon the blade.

'You wait out there all day?' a deep voice grumbled from within the cave.

Wraith took a step closer, Shatter still in hand, until the voice called out again.

'You don't need puny blade.'

Frustrated, Wraith sheathed the sword beneath her cloak, but kept a ready hand on the hilt. Her free hand rose to her chest and felt the arrowhead necklace beneath her armour, as was her custom for luck. She took a deep breath and entered the cave.

The cave was not particularly large, turning a single corner before opening up and revealing a small campsite. A fire burned in the centre, generating warmth and light as well as cooking a deer that hung over the flames. Tree logs were piled high, the occupant of the cave prepared against the cold of the mountains. The cavern floor was covered in more bones, rotting carcasses, and pieces of broken, rusted, and ruined armour.

Seated by the fire, with greyed skin, overgrown body, large drooping ears, bulbous nose, and broken fangs, was a troll. Its body was thin and feeble, weakened by starvation and far from the monstrous beast Wraith had been told so many stories of as a child.

The creature did not look to Wraith as she approached, focussed only on skinning the lamb in its brutish hands. A stone, bloodstained club leant against the wall of the cave behind the troll.

Her learnings with the Guild instantly came to mind. Trolls; distant kin of ogres, typically powerful and large, murderously furious, tough hides and basic weaponry paired with immense strength.

'What took you so long?' he grunted. 'Take seat over there. Warm self by fire.'

'You have a name?' Wraith asked as she sat upon the offered log of wood across the flames of the fire.

'Grak.'

'Do you know why I am here, Grak?'

'Course I do.' The troll continued with his work, undeterred by the newcomer. 'You Guild? Slayer?'

'I am.' She nodded.

'You not the first, nor will you be the last to hunt me.'

Yes, I will, Wraith thought.

'Found bodies of three sorcerers in the snow,' Grak said.

'Did you kill them?'

'No. Said found, not killed. Evil in land grows, planes shift, realms open.'

'I don't care,' Wraith said, the matters of the rest of the

realms of no concern as she looked to the troll, her contract, from across the fire.

'Farmers or shepherds pay you?' Grak asked.

'Both.'

'Punished for surviving.'

'Nobody's punishing you for surviving,' Wraith argued. 'You are wanted for taking and killing livestock...'

'Surviving!' he said with a raised voice. 'Not always like this. Had family and clan. Had home far from here. All taken. All gone. All burned away by humans and elves. Now here to hide. Here to survive.'

'It matters not,' Wraith said, though for a moment she felt pity for the beast. Her lessons and the rules returned to her. The contract. No more, no less.

'Family and clan mattered to me.' The troll grunted as he threw the now skinned lamb to the ground and then dragged enough towards the fire, beginning the process again.

'The thefts from the farmers and shepherds, they are not hiding,' Wraith said. 'Did you want this? Did you want my kind, Slayers, to hunt you?'

'Family and clan gone, hunted, yet still linger alone,' Grak admitted. 'Surviving, not living.'

'You know what will happen next?' Wraith gripped the hilts of the silver dagger and the shortsword hidden beneath her cloak. The familiar dull ache grew and spread within her hands.

'Warn you, won't be easy when time comes,' the troll vowed. 'Alone and old, still will not be easy for...'

The troll never finished his words as Wraith's silver dagger flew across the flames. The small blade struck true, tearing into Grak's neck, impaled in his throat. The troll coughed and spluttered dark blood as it struggled to stand, head striking the roof of the cave. Wraith moved quickly, rising from her seat with Shatter drawn and in hand. She leapt across the fire, knocking the roasting deer aside, and rammed the shortsword into Grak's chest, the troll's heart impaled. The creature staggered and collapsed to the cave floor, breath ragged before falling still.

'That was easy,' Wraith said to herself with uncertainty as she wrenched Shatter free of Grak's corpse, the blade coated in gore and blood. The Slayer reached for her silver dagger at the troll's throat, but stopped as Grak's eyes suddenly opened.

'Not... that... easy...' Grak spluttered as he clawed the silver dagger free.

Wraith watched in horror as the wounds from Shatter and the dagger healed before her eyes. Only acid and fire could kill a troll, she remembered. Backing away, she reached for the vials of acid hidden in her cloak and pulled them free. She meant to pour their liquid upon the blade of Shatter, but was forced to dive clear as Grak threw his stone club at the Slayer. The club barely missed the young woman, crashing into the cave wall and imbedding deep.

Wraith landed hard on the ground, the vials of acid falling from her grip and smashing upon the rock. She pulled quickly back as the acid hissed and burned harmlessly out of reach.

'Filthy medicines won't help you,' the troll sneered as it loomed over Wraith. He reached for her with large, foul fingers, blood and saliva dribbling from between rotten teeth.

Wraith lashed out with Shatter as she rolled away, the blade cutting at Grak's hand. The troll grunted, more from annoyance than pain. It grabbed a wooden log from the pile next to the fire and swung at the slayer. The blow caught Wraith across her face and chest, hitting like a hammer and throwing her farther across the cave. Dazed and seeing stars before her eyes, she reached out desperately for her fallen sword but found nothing. Her ears rang with the crescendo of bells. Blood ran down her chin from a split lip and dripped to the floor.

'Pathetic,' Grak grunted. 'Will bury when you die, not eat.'

Anger flooded through Wraith, and though she vowed she would not rely upon her hidden abilities this time, she reached out to call upon them. Her flames had saved her when hunting the siren and defeating the evil of Stonemere, but she took this contract to prove she was capable without them. Now she had no other choice. She reached out and tried to summon and unleash her arcane power... but nothing answered. No flicker of flame or even an ember emerged from her fingertips.

Grak just watched, puzzled, as Wraith reached out towards him with empty hands. The troll chuckled as he turned away from the slayer, and with a tremendous heave, pulled the stone club free of the cave wall.

'You best they send?' the monster teased and laughed as it used its club to stoke the flames of the campfire, thoughts returned to its meal rather than the slayer sent to kill him.

Wraith watched and waited as Grak threw another log onto the fire, letting its flames grow.

Acid and fire, she realised.

Recovering Shatter from the cave floor, Wraith turned on the troll, throwing a first, a second, and then her third and final dagger from beneath her cloak. All three struck the troll from behind, its back still turned on Wraith, seeing her as no threat. One of the daggers tore into the beast's back as the second and third struck behind the knee of the same leg. Grak buckled, staggering to one knee, head barely above the growing fire. Wraith sprinted towards her target and ran Shatter through the back of the unwounded knee.

Grak cried out and knelt over the fire, barely keeping balance as the flames rose towards his face.

'You are not the first to underestimate me,' Wraith told him as she wiped the blood from her chin, 'nor will you be the last.'

The kneeling troll swung wildly at the slayer, worsening his balance, but Wraith, using all the strength she possessed, barged Grak forward and onto the fires. The troll cried out in agony as the flames wrapped around him. He tried to force his way free, but the fire burned far quicker than it would upon the flesh of any other being; the trolls' greatest weakness. Wraith acted quickly, bringing Shatter down upon the outstretched hand of the troll, severing it just above the wrist, her proof of kill.

'Darkness... comes!' Grak shrieked as his body seared. 'None... safe! His... vengeance! Aaa... zzz... uurr... ootthh!'

Grak's screams fell silent as the fires fully engulfed and burned brightly, leaving Wraith alone. Her ears still rang horribly, but it was the troll's final word that haunted her. Axuroth.

CHAPTER TWO
THE CITY OF VARNHELM

Loyal, her black gelding thoroughbred, thankfully did not need instruction to lead them home and into the city. Wraith's face was already bruised and her ears still rang from the troll's beating. Her chest ached when she breathed deep, a rib or two likely cracked or broken, but there was a smile upon Wraith's face. The severed hand of the troll hung from her saddle alongside the sack of coin— payment from the farmers and shepherds bound for the Guild. It was not her first contract as a Slayer, but the first she had completed alone and without the flames of her hidden gift. It was her victory.

The guards at the gates to the city cleared the way the moment they saw her approach. They recognised Wraith, knowing her links to the Guild, and allowed her passage without questions, unlike all other arrivals. As she passed the gates, the city of Varnhelm, her home, welcomed her. The stench of the city and the hubbub of the very many people; it all brought a smile to her lips.

'You look like hell,' the familiar voice of a she-elf called from atop the battlements.

'I feel it too,' Wraith replied, despite her still-present smile.

She saw a shadow move quickly across the battlements of Varnhelm before dropping down to a building's roof, then a lower roof, and then down to the road ahead. The agility was impressive, but expected from an elf, especially this one.

Beneath the raised hood were youthful, slender features, blue eyes, long brown hair, and pointed ears burnt at their tips. A pair of curved knives was sheathed at her belt. The elf eyed the rider with a narrowed, scornful glare.

'Waiting eagerly for my return, Raven?' Wraith asked with a cheeky smile.

'Waiting to see if you returned at all,' she said sternly. 'You should not have gone without me, and certainly not alone.'

'That was the point.'

'I guessed as much.' Raven fell into step beside Loyal, patting the horse's neck. 'I had a mind to follow you, as did the Guildmaster.'

'Yet you did not.'

'Did I need to?' Raven asked.

'No.'

'The bruises on your face beg to differ.'

'The slain hand of a troll says otherwise,' Wraith said confidently.

'You did not seek us out,' Raven said. 'Not me, the wolf, nor the bandit.'

'To prove I could do this alone,' the Slayer said. 'No allies, no tricks, and no… flames.'

'There is no need to prove anything. Your actions at Stonemere attest to that.'

'Regardless,' Wraith said with a sigh, 'it was good to do this one alone.'

Raven nodded in acceptance. The pair continued through the city, passing the various districts of Varnhelm. One trader offered them glittering necklaces and rings, whilst another displayed his variety of ornately decorated swords, and a seamstress displayed her finest materials and wares. A ragged man, head and hands fixed in the stocks, flashed the Slayer and elf a toothless grin. A priestess of Halim slowly crossed the street ahead of them, eyes white with blindness, though it seemed the Gods were leading her way as she clutched holy symbols in her hands.

The sun was setting in the distance, and as the merchants of the Crafts and Trade districts were closing for the day, the Entertainment and Ale districts were beginning to come to life with singers, performers, and already a few drunken louts.

'How go things at the Guild?' Wraith asked as they approached the Governance District and their home.

'In the two days you've been away?' Raven chuckled. 'Much as it always is. Arguments between assassins and slayers over who gets what assignment. New contracts come in daily, faster than the Guild can complete them. Apprentices continue to be trained, though news reached us that a handful on their trials had fallen…'

'Any word on Luthor?' Wraith asked of her friend when she was but an apprentice. Wraith and Luthor had set out in different directions on their trials, their rites of passage to earn membership to the Guild. Whereas Wraith and others had returned, Luthor had remained missing and unheard of.

'Nothing,' Raven said with remorse. 'I think any hope of his return has now faded. He is lost to us. I am sorry.'

'Luthor was a friend to me when I was first brought

here. Marek always said Luthor was not cut out for this life. Perhaps he was right after all.'

'The realms of Centuros are a dangerous place, though I long to see more of them now I've had a taste.'

'Me too.' Wraith smiled in agreement.

They continued through the city and soon were beneath the towering structures of the Governance District. There, noble families and highborns went about their business, none giving the Slayer or elf a second glance. A young boy was pulled away from their path and warned not to go near those of the Guild. The boy dared to look back to Wraith and Raven and stuck his tongue out in defiance. Wraith laughed, but Raven pulled a damning, furious face, making the boy scamper in fright.

'What?' the elf laughed as Wraith laughed more in surprise and disbelief.

Ahead of them was their destination, the stone keep of the Guild. The fortification, the oldest structure in sight, was as striking to Wraith as it was the first time she saw it eight years ago. The stone towers, battlements, and gargoyles were imposing amongst the grander and finer buildings of the District. Wraith dismounted and removed the troll's hand and the sack of coins from the saddle at the stairs that led up to entrance doors. A blind boy approached and took the reins of Loyal, leading the horse towards the Guild's stables. Wraith had tried many times to speak to the boy, who had not aged in all her time of living in Varnhelm, but never had she heard a response.

Together, Wraith and Raven climbed the stone stairs where at the summit awaited two stone statues. As the Slayer and elf neared, the heads of the stone statues turned to look upon the newcomers. Their gaze lingered for a moment, before the wooden doors to the keep creaked open and the statue heads returned to facing forward.

'Who goes there?' muttered a harsh voice from the darkness within the keep.

'Agron, it's me, Raven,' the elf said with annoyance. 'I'm here with Wraith, Slayer, and guild-member.'

'Prove it,' the voice demanded.

Wraith lifted her sleeve to reveal the branding at her wrist, the intricately designed arrowhead formed of a roaring beast, poisoned dagger, silhouette, and locked box.

'Hmph... enter... but I warn you, no funny business.'

As Wraith and Raven entered the keep, they were greeted by the hulking, tattooed, and grey-skinned form of a barbarian, likely of the Skypeak Mountain Tribes. Scars covered his arms and bare chest, and he awaited the pair with arms crossed and axe in hand.

'Bored already, Agron?' Raven asked as they passed the barbarian.

'Yes,' he admitted with a grunt. 'I just want to break something... or someone... anything!'

'I'm sure someone will upset the Guildmaster soon enough,' Wraith said.

'Someone already has.' Agron threw his axe down upon a table and slumped into a seat.

'Who?'

'You'll see,' he said with a nod towards the stairs.

Wraith and Raven hurried up the staircase beyond the bored barbarian and quickly reached the upper levels of the Guild. Through a creaking oak door, they entered the dimly lit hall that was the inn of the Guild. What they expected to find was the usual crowd of those drinking and feasting, with many gathered and likely arguing around the contract wall. Instead, what they found was a half empty hall with the only occupants gathered in a tight-knit group. From amongst the huddled group, voices

17

were raised, shouting and arguing, the loudest of all belonging to the Guildmaster.

'Silence, I command it!' he called, but only half the voices hushed.

Near fifty years of age with grey amongst his dark hair, age lines upon his face, along with other scars and tokens of battle. Hazel eyes, just like the apprentice's, looked to the gathering with authority and anger. He wore armour with his sword sheathed at his side and hand gripped tight around the hilt. His name was Brevik Duskrun, the Guildmaster.

'HE SAID SILENCE!' roared a towering half-orc with a white beard, dark green skin, and tusks for teeth. He had been the sole guard of the keep for many years, but now acted as the Guildmaster's bodyguard, the role vacated by Raven. All fell silent in the hall at the half-orcs angered command.

'Thank you, Klunt,' Brevik said.

'What's going on?' Wraith asked as she and Raven approached, but the Guildmaster did not answer.

'Punishment is what's happening here!' cheered Juredny Ironbreaker, female dwarf and slayer of beasts, from amongst the assembly.

'Punishment?' cried a voice. 'For what?'

At the centre of the crowd, seated whilst all others stood, was a weasel-faced, pox-scarred halfling. At his wrist was the guild branding. The locked box was most prominent, marking the halfling as a thief of the guild. Wraith recognised him, a guild-member for two or three years, by the name of Limso Murnelly.

'I don't see what the problem is,' the halfling protested. 'I completed the contract, retrieving the…'

'Enough, Limso,' Brevik ordered sternly, then looked to all those gathered, and then lastly to Wraith. 'What are our rules? All of you, what are rules?'

'Fulfil the contract. No more, no less,' all recited, even Limso.

'Two?'

'Do nothing without payment. There is a cost for everything.'

'Three?'

'No bloodshed within the Guild. Outside is a different story.'

'And lastly?'

'Any who shame the Guild will be punished.'

'And do you understand the penalty for breaking our rules?' the Guildmaster asked.

'Punishment,' all but Limso said.

'What was your contract, Limso?' Brevik asked.

'Steal the blood ruby amulet from the Tween family manor,' the halfling said.

'And what did you leave with?'

'The amulet…'

'What else?' the Guildmaster demanded.

'Nothing… I…'

'Don't lie to me!' Brevik ordered.

'WHAT ELSE?' roared Klunt as the half-orc brought his axe down between the halfling's legs, narrowly missing anything of importance. Limso's skin paled, eyes wide with fear.

'Two… two pearl earrings,' Limso confessed.

Wraith, Raven, and all those gathered let out a collective groan.

'At last the truth,' Brevik said.

'They were just sitting there on the dresser amongst all the rest of Lady Tween's jewellery,' Limso tried to explain. 'I didn't think they'd notice.'

'What is rule one?' the Guildmaster asked of the

halfling.

'Fulfil the contract. No more, no less.'

Brevik sighed with disappointment. 'Do you understand the penalty?'

Limso looked from Brevik to Klunt's axe between his legs and then back again. The halfling then looked to the branding at his wrist.

'I do,' he finally said.

'Uluma?' Brevik called out.

'About time,' a voice muttered from a darkened corner of the hall.

Uluma Dadin, cleric and servant of the God Halim, the devout and holy. The halfling sat with her leg resting on the table, draining her tankard of ale before belching and then looking over the gathering. From her neck hung the tarnished and worn symbol of Halim, a sun shining through the clouds.

'Right, let's see this done and over with,' she muttered, dropping the tankard to the table and stumbling towards the Guildmaster.

'No… no… you don't have to do this…' Limso panicked.

The Guildmaster ignored the halfling's pleas and nodded to Klunt. As Raven and Juredny Ironbreaker held Limso down to his chair with arm held out, the half-orc raised his axe. The thief fought against them in an attempt to flee, but he was held firmly in place.

'Limso Murnelly,' Brevik addressed the seated halfling. 'You have brought shame to this Guild. Your thieving hands led you to this fate. Now you will lose one, as punishment.'

At that final word, the axe came down and severed the arm just above the wrist. The halfling screamed as blood spurted from the wound.

'Uluma,' Brevik instructed, no pride or happiness in his voice as he looked down upon the ruin of Limso's severed hand on the floor.

'Halim, I call upon you now,' the cleric chanted as her hand reached out and settled on Limso's shoulder. Light emanated from the sun symbol of Halim about the cleric's neck as it glowed warmly. 'Bestow your favour. Guide us towards your light.'

Limso's cries fell silent as the healer's light took hold of him. The wound at his arm stopped bleeding and then began to close until it was a ruined, scarred stump.

'Disrespect me and this Guild again, and it will be your head next time,' Brevik warned before turning his back on the thief, and those gathered began to disperse. Klunt cleaned his axe, Juredny Ironbreaker ordered a tankard, and several of the others approached the contract wall, looking for work. The Guildmaster then tossed a large bronze coin, a Guild marker, to Uluma as payment and thanks.

'Been in the wars again, girl?' Uluma greeted as she approached Wraith.

'I'm fine,' the Slayer lied, despite the pain in her chest and face inflicted by the troll's wrath.

'Your face says different,' the cleric joked, slapping a warm hand on Wraith's back. Instantly, the pain lessened, and even the ringing in her ears was gone.

'Thank you,' Wraith tried to say, but already the healer had walked away, ordering another ale.

'Not dead yet?' Klunt called to Wraith.

'Not yet.' She smiled. 'Enjoying your new job?'

'Use my axe more now,' the half-orc sneered.

'I think Brevik prefers his old bodyguard,' Wraith remarked, seeing Raven and the Guildmaster in quiet conversation. 'Does he miss her?'

'Not that he'd ever admit.' Klunt sniffed the air. 'Why do I smell troll?'

'Because I've been hunting one.' Wraith lifted the severed hand of the troll to view.

'And so the slayer returns with contract complete,' Brevik said as he and Raven approached.

'One dead troll and coin for payment,' Wraith replied as she handed over the farmer's sack of coin. 'The Guild's cut.'

Brevik placed three Guild markers in Wraith's hand, large bronze coins, each marked with the Guild symbols of beast, dagger, silhouette, and locked box, all forming an arrowhead matching the brand upon the guild members' wrists.

The Guildmaster then looked to the troll's hand before looking to the Slayer with doubt.

'Fire?' he questioned.

'Only fire and acid can kill a troll,' she replied.

'Fire?' he repeated.

'His own, as fate would have it.' She forced the sack of coin into his hands.

'All of you,' Brevik called out to those in the hall. 'This is how you complete a contract. Proof and payment.'

A few faces looked on with approval, but one was certainly jealous and scornful.

'Of course you'd praise her,' Limso Murnelly sneered as he rose to stand, cradling his brutalized arm. 'She was always your favourite, even when just an apprentice.'

'Hold your tongue,' Raven warned him.

'Who are you?' the halfling scoffed. 'You don't have a brand? You are not of the Guild.'

'Oh, I have a brand and I swore no one would ever mark me in such a way again,' Raven replied as her hands fell to her sheathed curved knives.

'Hey.' Wraith stepped between the pair and looked down at the halfling. 'What is your problem?'

'I wonder,' he spat, raising his barely healed stump in anger.

'Limso, you've taken your punishment, now leave it at that,' Guildmaster Brevik cautioned.

'Careful, halfling, or I'll take your other hand too,' Klunt warned.

'No, let him speak,' Wraith encouraged. 'What is your grievance with me?'

'The Stonemere contract should never have gone to you,' the thief protested. 'It called for a Saviour, not a Slayer, yet you took it as your very first assignment, before any of us had the chance. Now, as the mighty *Wraith*, your name and deeds defeating the scourge of Stonemere have spread beyond Varnhelm already, though few of us believe them.'

'What do you mean?'

'The tales the bards spread about you and your group the Forsaken entertain sure enough, though hold little truth,' he said with a sly smile. 'I am not alone in thinking our Guildmaster's favour has led to this praise. After all, is it not true that the blade you carry was, in fact, gifted by our very own Brevik Duskrun? Can you be surprised there are those of us who believe you just might be the secret daughter of our Guildmaster, birthed from some poor wench...'

'You little...' Brevik raged with a raised fist.

'Wait,' Wraith said, stopping the Guildmaster before looking around her to the other guild members. 'Are there others here who doubt my worth?'

A low murmur crept across the hall, no voices or words clear to understand, but certainly vocal enough to show that there were those in agreement.

'What is it you want, Limso? I completed the Stone-mere contract and now this assignment, slaying a troll that was raiding farmlands…'

'A sickly, wretched thing by the looks of that,' the halfling sneered at the troll's hand.

'As good a condition as yours,' joked Raven, drawing Limso's ire again.

'What is it you want?' Wraith asked, wanting to get to the point. 'I have nothing to prove to you or any other.'

'Take a contract of my choosing,' the halfling suggested. 'Not one hand-picked by our revered Guildmaster.'

'You don't have to do this…' Brevik began.

'No.' Wraith stopped him. 'Go on, Limso. If that's what it takes to shut you up, lead on. Go to the contract wall and find me an assignment.'

The halfling shuffled away towards the wall covered in parchments, any in his way quickly stepping aside as all eyes were on the confrontation.

'You don't have to prove yourself, least of all to him,' Raven assured.

'If I must prove myself again, so be it,' Wraith replied before following Limso to the contract wall. 'So, what be it, halfling? What challenge do you suggest?'

Limso looked up to the many pieces of parchment that covered the wall, each marked by a symbol of the Guild for slayers, assassins, saviours, and thieves. Each a different contract, a different assignment sent to the Guild for completion by its members. Wraith waited as the halfling looked over the many postings before his eyes settled upon one, a cunning smile spreading across his lips.

'This one,' Limso stated, pointing up to a worn, tattered page. The assignment had been posted many months ago, its description and reward changed repeatedly. It was the only posting upon the wall that was marked by not one

Guild symbol, but by the symbols of all four professions; the slayer, saviour, assassin, and thief. 'Lockwood Mausoleum,' the halfling said aloud for all to hear. A murmur spread across the hall, this time of shock and disbelief.

'No,' Brevik intervened. 'No, Limso. You hold no power here and can force no one to take an assignment against their will.'

The voices around the hall murmured again and Wraith knew the rumours of favouritism were gaining momentum with Brevik's defence. She caught Raven's eye, the elf shaking her head in warning.

'I'll take it,' Wraith declared, reaching forward and tearing the parchment from the wall.

A low cheer sounded around her, while others protested and laughed. Raven and Brevik looked on in dismay.

'Enough! Show's over,' Brevik ordered, the members of the guild returning to their own business.

'How you going to help her this time?' Limso sneered.

'He doesn't have to,' Wraith vowed.

'You don't know what you've done, girl.' He chuckled with sinister intent.

'Limso, clean up the mess you left behind,' the Guild-master ordered, pointing to the puddle of blood where the halfling had sat and received his punishment. 'Your hand is still twitching.'

CHAPTER THREE
THE GUILD

THE CITY OF VARNHELM

'You don't know what you've done.' Brevik repeated the halfling thief's words. The Guildmaster was pacing around his study, still fuming at Limso Murnelly's challenge. Wraith and Raven were seated, the elf inspecting the rare collection of artefacts, weapons, and armour whilst the slayer warmed herself by the fire in the hearth.

'I don't see what the big deal is,' Wraith argued as she looked at the parchment again. 'Viscount Lakewood…'

'Lockwood,' Raven corrected as she poured herself a large goblet of fine wine and drank deep.

'Viscount Lockwood, thank you,' Wraith continued, 'seeks the return of an ancestral relic from his family's mausoleum in the grounds of the abandoned fortress of Karnock. I go there, enter a crypt, and find his family… whatever… and return it home. I don't see why that poses such a challenge.'

'And what if I told you that particular contract has been upon the wall for near six months now,' Brevik said.

'No one has dared enter the mausoleum?'

'Oh, they have,' Brevik replied.

'Many of them,' Raven added, drinking deep of her goblet again and then picking up an ogre skull from the desk and juggling it between her hands.

'That's why the reward has risen so many times,' Brevik said.

'And why it is open to all Guild members, no matter their profession?' the elf asked.

Wraith looked to the parchment again and saw that across its bottom were all the guild symbols. The silhouette of a missing person and the requirement for a Saviour. A roaring beast and the need for a Slayer. A dagger dripping with poison, a target for an Assassin. The locked box needing a Thief.

'A missing person needing assassination, locked in a box guarded by a monster?' Wraith joked.

'This isn't funny,' Brevik warned. 'You've accepted a challenge and taken a contract that has claimed the lives of everyone who has attempted it. You now need to see it completed. Limso is only doing this as retribution to me and my punishment, and for that, I am sorry.'

'Which he rightly deserved,' Raven added.

'Maybe he was right,' Wraith suggested. 'You have been lenient to me.'

'Family tends to do that,' he said regretfully, 'despite best intentions. I can't be seen to be helping you.'

'Nor would I want it. There are already too many suspicions.'

Limso was wrong, but close with his guess that she was Brevik's daughter. *Too close.*

'You will need help,' the Guildmaster advised. 'No going alone like you did with the troll.'

'I know some who I may be able to interest in joining me,'

Wraith said, looking to Raven. There was doubt and concern in the elf's eyes, but eventually she nodded in agreement.

'Of course,' Raven said. 'I know two fellows in the Coin who will join us, willing and unwilling.'

'Your Forsaken,' Brevik realised. 'And what of a certain fiend apprentice in the Sacred?'

'Acolyte,' Wraith corrected. 'I haven't seen Jakseyth since Stonemere, but I could send a letter to the citadel.'

'Yes… yes, perhaps this is not such a tragedy after all,' Brevik said. 'If you could complete the Lockwood Mausoleum contract… well, the renown and fame that comes with that would be beyond anything we have achieved so far in Varnhelm.'

'A pity it is us who have to do all the work,' Raven snapped at him. The elf was one of the few people who could speak to the Guildmaster like that, their bond going back to before Wraith was taken in by the Guild.

'This could achieve attention from the capital of Aelthorn,' Brevik said as he poured himself a goblet of fine wine. 'The Lockwoods were a prominent noble house before their fall, even holding the ear of royalty. Maybe the court of King Rothgard will hear of the tale.'

'Enough,' Raven implored. 'Rumour has it Rothgard doesn't dare leave his palace, let alone deal with the likes of us.'

'I must look to the future.'

'Even if your ambition claims your niece?'

'Keep your voice down. You know we do not want that particular information to be public knowledge. Already there are those who suspect I favour her.'

'About Stonemere…' Wraith said with concern as she stopped the bickering pair. 'When I cornered the troll in the Skypeaks, his last word was *Axuroth*.'

'Axuroth?' Raven questioned. 'That's the name we kept seeing and hearing in Stonemere.'

'And that village was near torn apart by monstrosities.'

'Enough. Enough, both of you,' Brevik ordered. 'This is not the business of you or the Guild. This was the Sacred's concern, not ours. You above all people do not want the Sacred's attention any more than you already do. I do not want to hear that name again.'

'But…' Wraith began.

'Alena!' Brevik said firmly, using her real name, something he swore not to do due to the danger it could place them both in. 'I have worked hard to make this guild what it is, and that is only thanks to following the rules I set in stone and demand all members follow. Earlier with Limso shows cracks in our foundations and my own failings. I will not allow you to suffer his fate. I am sorry, but this conversation is over. Forget you ever heard the name Axuroth.'

'Fine,' Wraith said, rising from her seat. 'I will seek out the Suppliers, our fellows at the Coin, and then head out for Karnock.'

'Already?' Raven questioned. 'You only just returned.'

'No point in postponing.'

'And so Wraith and her Forsaken venture out again,' Brevik said with a hint of pride. 'I do not need to say this, but do be careful out there. There is a reason no one has returned from the Lockwood crypts. I recommend seeking out the viscount. He resides in the city of Rheins, south of Karnock.'

'I will,' she said as she approached the door.

'Wraith.' Brevik stopped her. 'I apologise for being hard on you before. I am only looking out for you.'

'As you always do.'

Thank you, Uncle, she thought as she left Raven and Brevik in the study.

———

The first supplier she approached was the Armourer in the Crafts District.

The heat of the forge struck the moment Wraith stepped into his workplace. She passed the mass collections of weaponry and armours, enough to equip an army twice over. There were many blades, axes, shields, and plated pieces of armour that would cost hundreds of golden coins to purchase, the craftsmanship finer than that seen in much of the realms. It was here that her own armour—leather inlaid with chainmail—was crafted. Normally, master-smith Thainin Thunderhorn would be at work at the forge, creating his latest masterpiece, striking hammer to heated iron. Now though, the forge was unmanned, heated coals and tools awaiting, yet no armourer. She would need to return later when Thainin was at work again.

Second was the Scholar, hidden away in his small library in the Governance District.

As always, his chambers smelt old and forgotten. Two dozen bookcases housed tombs, scrolls, and piles of parchments. Maps of the realms and their continents and countries covered several walls, whilst sketches and details of monsters and beasts covered others. There were more piles and stacks of books and papers in all directions, and amongst them, Wraith found the young gnome, Tanbar Alryn.

'Hello, hello,' the gnome greeted as he peered through thick lenses. 'Pleased to be seeing you once again. How can I be helping you today?'

'Everything you know of the Karnock Fortress and the Lockwood Mausoleum,' she asked, placing a single guild marker upon his desk.

He looked to her with doubt at first, and then fear.

'Are you certain?' Tanbar asked.

'Absolutely,' Wraith replied, though his concern brought further doubts to her mind.

For all these people to be concerned, is this one beyond me?

Tanbar hurried away, rifling through the bookcases, but quickly returned with books, scrolls, and a map he had drawn out himself.

'You are not the first to ask of this location,' the scholar said.

'So I understand,' Wraith replied, tempted to ask how many had come before her before deciding ignorance would be better.

'Karnock Fortress rests in the north-east of our nation of Castille,' Tanbar explained. 'The Lockwoods were one of the first noble houses in Castille. Their fortress of Karnock guarded the eastern pass through the Skypeak Mountains and was the site of some of the fiercest battles in the Dark Days when they stood against the chaos wrought by mages.'

The Dark Days was what many called the time when warring sorcerers ruled the lands and enslaved its people. It was only thanks to the emergence of the Sacred that the murderous warlords were vanquished and the lands freed. The Dark Days were over, though there were those who believed the Sacred were as much oppressors as any of the fallen warlords.

'Karnock has been abandoned for several decades and fallen into ruin,' the gnome continued. 'The Lockwoods and any survivors fleeing south.'

'Why did it fall to ruin?' Wraith asked, thinking of her own forgotten home so long ago.

'It is not known for certain, though there are rumours.'

'Such as?'

'That it was purged by the Sacred and the Lockwood family left to ruin.'

'They've recovered well enough, it seems,' Wraith said. 'The contract was written by a viscount of the family.'

'Viscount Christoph Lockwood,' Tanbar confirmed. 'The viscount has returned some pride to his family, though they remain divided and bickering. Rumours persist of the viscount's... honourability.'

'Like all lords in power I have come across. What can you tell me of the Lockwood Mausoleum?'

'Few details are known.' Tanbar handed over a roughly drawn out map copied from a faded scroll. 'The mausoleum is a vast crypt beneath the fortress, with four entrances from the main courtyard. This is the original design, though I expect it has changed in all these years. What is shown is only the upper levels.'

'And I bet I will have to descend farther than that to find what I need,' Wraith said. 'Any suggestion of defences?'

'Traps?' Tanbar said. 'Not on the plans, but you can be certain the Lockwoods have defended their ancestors well. What is it you seek within the mausoleum? None who have sought information of the fortress have been able to tell me, nor have any returned.'

'I will seek out those very details from the Lockwoods in Rheins. Perhaps they can help with details of the lower levels too.'

The scholar set himself to work quickly, and within mere moments, he had produced a map of the journey from Varnhelm to Rheins and then to the ruined fortress of Karnock. Despite the short time, the map possessed a surprising amount of detail.

Wraith placed another marker on the gnome's desk.

'Thank you,' she said, but before she could leave, Tanbar spoke one last time.

'Do be careful out there,' he said. 'It would pain the heart if you did not return.'

Next was the Alchemist, Wraith venturing into the dangerous slums of the city. She felt eyes upon her instantly, and her hand remained on the crimson hilt of Shatter.

Wraith opened the door to the small shop but only managed to take a single step inside before a mighty blast swept her off her feet and she tumbled back. Her head was dazed and her ears were ringing once again. Coughing and spluttering, she struggled to her feet, waving the smoke from her face.

'Wooooee!' cheered a woman's voice from the thick fog clouding the air. 'That one packed a helluva punch.'

Wraith staggered inside, waving the smoke clear ahead of her and trying not to breathe in deep of the foulness. The shop was a mess, worse than usual. Tables, cauldrons, and broken wood and glass littered the floor. Chemicals and powders of all colours and stenches were scattered in all directions, and Wraith took care not to step on any of it.

The alchemist, Juzinta Oscal, smiled madly as she patted out the remaining flames on her overalls. Her hair was as wild as ever, stained crimson, black, and purple, though a section at the scalp was missing. Cuts and burns marked her face, and her overalls and gloves were torn, revealing bleeding wounds beneath.

'Do you need to see a healer?' Wraith asked.

'Oh, no. No, thank you,' Juzinta said, waving away the concern as she still grinned manically. 'My experiments have done far worse to me before and likely will again. Anyway, what can I help you with today, dearie?'

'Just replacement vials of acid,' Wraith said with a raised Guild marker. 'I still have the three healing potions and a pair of antidotes.'

'What happened to the acid you purchased previously?' Juzinta asked with a crazed look. 'Did you put it to use giving the troll a grizzly, melting end?'

'Not quite.' Wraith chuckled, not wanting to admit she accidentally dropped the vials, losing them pointlessly.

'Fine, fine, fine. Keep the gory details to yourself,' the alchemist said as she hurried to her fallen and broken cabinets that had been thrown by the blast. From inside, she removed two still intact small green vials. 'As per the last, these will burn flesh but not the steel of your blades. With them, you have utterly cleaned out my stock for the time being.'

The alchemist offered the two bottles of acid, but Wraith backed away, gesturing at the table. Wraith was not being rude, but she did not want to touch whatever foul liquids and powders covered the alchemist's gloves. She rested the Guild marker on the table and took the acid, securing the vials away in her cloak.

'Next time we must find you something… more interesting, dearie,' Juzinta said.

'Next time try, not to blow us, or the entire keep, up in smoke.'

'One can only try. But I tell you what, for an extra marker, I can give you something that will certainly help give you an edge when your back is against the wall.'

She placed a single small vial upon the table, a milky white fluid with shimmering flakes inside.

'Use it only when you have no other choice,' the Alchemist advised with a drinking motion.

'Thank you.' Wraith wanted to ask more, but already the Alchemist was mixing more chemicals and threatening another explosion.

Last of all was the Fence, his deceitful business found in the Trade District.

The shop housed a fine collection of rare items, artefacts, and trophies. Crystals and gems sparkled in the light, as did other tokens of fortune. Upon stands and housed in glass displays were weapons, pieces of armour, an array of rings and amulets, and even a shimmering cloak, all possessing a measure of the arcane.

Behind a collection of bracers and helms stood the Fence, Vimo Vistelo, a human with a tongue of silver that could charm its way almost anywhere. He wore an open purple shirt with a blue waistcoat, always dressed in the finer things. Between the bejewelled, ringed fingers of a hand twirled a Guild marker.

Vimo was not alone. With the Fence stood the Armourer, Thainin Thunderhorn. The dwarven smith and crafter with powerful muscular arms was completely bald with a typically long and thick dwarven beard. His skin and overalls were darkened and stained by ash and sweat. In his strong hands was a knife, the hilt a golden skeleton draped in a shroud.

'The ritual blade from Stonemere,' Wraith said as she approached.

'Just the one.' Vimo smiled widely. 'Welcome, my dear Slayer. Do you recognise this token from your exploits?'

'I remember it stabbing me,' she replied, with a hand to her stomach.

'How went your tangle with the troll?' Thainin asked.

'I'm still standing, just. I'm heading out on another contract soon...'

'The Lockwood Mausoleum,' Vimo said with a

knowing look. 'Word spreads quickly. You sure are a brave one to be tackling that.'

'Yeah…' Wraith looked back at the dwarf. 'I wanted to see you for…'

'Repairs?' Thainin guessed.

'And to purchase more throwing daggers.'

'Again?' he asked with dismay. 'How many this time?'

'Make it four.'

'Leave your armour and blades at my forge,' the dwarf instructed. 'You heading for the Recruiter's Coin before leaving? I will have your belongings brought there as soon as ready.'

'Thank you,' Wraith said, handing over a Guild marker. 'So what have you learned of that knife since I brought it back?'

'Very little,' Thainin admitted. 'The knife is old, centuries old, but still strong. The design on the hilt hints at cult usage. It was not forged by men, elves, or dwarves, and certainly not by any skill I have seen, just like that shortsword of yours.'

'Shatter,' Wraith replied.

'Yes,' the dwarf said. 'I would be keen to spend time giving that particular blade a closer look too.'

'One day,' Wraith looked to the ritual knife. 'For now, what about this one?'

'I cannot help there.'

'And that is precisely why you have brought this fascinating item to me,' Vimo said with joy as he lifted the knife out of the dwarf's hands. He held the blade to the light and inspected it closely. 'A fine specimen,' he commented. 'Let's see what secrets you hold.'

Vimo's blue eyes flickered and flashed golden with arcane energy. He breathed deep and then spoke calm and slow. 'A history of blood and death. This goes back to

36

before the Dark Days. The lives it has taken... the inno-cents... its origin is...'

Vimo recoiled, horror on his face as he dropped the knife to the ground. His eyes clamped shut, the arcane fading as he stepped away. 'Take that thing away from here,' the Fence ordered as Thainin recovered it from the floor.

'What did you see?' the dwarf and Wraith both asked.

'Evil,' was all Vimo could say, horrified.

'Axuroth?' Wraith tried. 'Does that name mean anything to you?'

Vimo's look of shock confirmed her suspicions. 'I know not why, but that name was uttered throughout the blade's dark history.' He shook his head with a scornful gaze.

Vimo turned away and pulled a flask from his waist-coat, drinking deep of a strong liquor within.

'I apologise. I lost my composure for a moment,' he said. 'Thainin, my old friend. Please remove that blade from my sight. I do not wish to ever lay eyes upon it.'

'Thank you for trying,' the Armourer said with concern as he covered the ritual knife in a cloth. 'Wraith, I will have your equipment sent to you at the Coin when ready.'

'What will you do with it?' she asked, looking to concealed knife.

'Hide it away for now,' Thainin said. 'It is likely for the best that we all forget about it.'

The Armourer nodded his thanks to Vimo again before departing.

'So, my dear Slayer,' Vimo said as he lit a pipe and blew rings of smoke into the air, 'now those troubles are behind us, can I interest you in anything from my fine collection? Perhaps a cloak of the falcon, gifting transformation into a bird of prey? Or cursed robes of the inferno, incinerating whoever wears them. Maybe just something small, like a ring of protection or amulet of striking. You may find in the depths of Lockwood Mausoleum that you are in need of an edge.'

'Not now, Vimo,' Wraith said. 'I still need to earn a lot more markers to afford any of your prized possessions.'

'Complete the Lockwood contract and you will not find markers in short supply. I understand it was the halfling Limso Murnelly who challenged you. That thief has always had a big mouth... big eyes too, and far too greedy.'

'He brought those stolen goods to you, didn't he?'

'How do you think your Guildmaster discovered the betrayal?' He chuckled.

'Until next time, Vimo.'

'You are always welcome, my girl,' he replied with a pleasing grin. 'Until next time, Slayer. Good luck out there.'

CHAPTER FOUR
THE RECRUITER'S COIN INN

THE CITY OF VARNHELM

With her preparations complete and armaments being repaired and refined by Thainin Thunderhorn, Wraith made her way to the Ale District. From atop Loyal, she saw groups drunkenly singing and cheering, a knight trying to win the heart of a maiden, and two pregnant women chasing after a terrified man. It brought a smile to Wraith's lips, seeing the lives, triumphs, and even the miseries of the people around her. It was normal life, something she had missed out on thanks to fate and the loss of her home and family. Now, the Guild was all she knew and had.

At the heart of the district, amongst the stinking streets already crowded with patrons, was the Recruiter's Coin Inn. Wraith tied Loyal's reins in the stables, took a deep breath, and then headed inside. As always, the inn was busy and loud. A crowd of dwarves was singing at the top of their voices, cheering for their kill of a hydra. A singer recounted a haunting ballad in one corner as another led a cheery jig. As always, the heads and skulls of beasts of all species lined the walls above the patrons, trophies alongside armour, shields and flags displaying nations and armies.

'Make way, my fellow, for I see we have a Wraith amongst us,' called a voice from behind the bar. It was Kiplan, the young and handsome barkeeper, with unbuttoned shirt, green eyes, blonde curls, and short beard. He smiled at Wraith and beckoned her closer. Already seated on a stool at his side, with a cup of wine in hand, was Raven.

'Took your time.' She mumbled before taking a long drink of her cup.

'Almost ready,' Wraith replied. 'The other two here?'

'Oh, yes.'

'They know where I'm headed?'

'Where *we're* headed,' Raven corrected before drinking again. 'And no. They know we are leaving soon, but I didn't tell them the destination. I didn't want to scare them off.'

'You all right?' Wraith asked.

'Not exactly thrilled at the idea of where we are headed.'

'The crypts?' Wraith asked before realising the truth of it. *She doesn't want to go underground.*

'My kind, we… I won't fare well down there.'

'I understand,' Wraith said. 'You don't have to come with me.'

'Then what kind of bodyguard would I be?' Raven chuckled.

'You're not my bodyguard.'

'Regardless…' the elf took a deep breath and another swig of wine. 'I'll be at your side.'

'You don't have to…'

'Enough. It is decided,' Raven vowed. 'Kiplan, another cup. Actually, just bring me the bottle.'

'Here you go, Raven,' the handsome barkeep said with bottle in hand. 'Go easy on this. It's strong.'

'It's for the ride to our next challenge,' the elf replied. 'And as we enter the crypts. In fact, give me a second bottle. I think I'll need it.'

She pulled a handful of silver from a pouch, but Wraith stopped her, handing over three gold coins.

'You're drinking this because of me. The least I can do is pay.' The Slayer handed over the coins to Kiplan. 'Do I owe anything else for Fenrix?'

'Not at all,' he replied. 'He earns his keep and minds his manners, unlike others I could name.'

'The bandit?' Raven guessed correctly.

'Fenrix had any trouble?' Wraith asked, not wanting to know of the troubles Quinlan had caused.

'We've certainly had some strange patrons here, and he's among them,' Kiplan replied. 'He's had more than his fair share of trouble, but no more than any half-orc or fiend that comes through here. He's even helped me out a few times when ruffians crossed the line with the working girls. When needed, I've kept an eye out for him.'

'Thank you,' Wraith said.

'Never a problem.' He offered a charming smile that made Wraith blush.

'You spinning another coin today?' he asked, meaning the practice and ritual of recruiting followers for a venture by spinning a coin on the bar.

'I'm just here for Fenrix and Quinlan,' she replied.

'By the hearth last I saw them,' the barkeep said.

Wraith left the bar and crossed the inn. Sure enough, seated at a table near the hearth was Quinlan Vespasian Clysley the Fourth. Dressed in a fine yet repaired waistcoat and jacket with high collar, with slicked back blonde hair, grey eyes, and an ever-present smile to match his charm.

He sat across from a grizzled dwarf, cards in hand and coins bet upon the table. At his side was seated a young lass, bosom straining against the fabric of her dress, eyes looking to the highborn with adoration.

'Your turn, my good fellow,' he said in his a noble tone.

'Show me your cards,' his dwarven opponent said as he tossed a silver coin to the table.

'There you go,' Quinlan cheered with a broad smile as he laid out his cards. 'Full court! Nothing can beat that!'

'Can't be,' sneered the dwarf with dismay that became anger. 'You cheated! I was warned I shouldn't play you!'

'All is fair when the cards are drawn,' Quinlan said innocently, with one hand raised and the other kept under the table.

'There's nothing fair about this!' the dwarf spat as he drew a dagger. 'I'll kill you sooner than see you take my coin!'

'ENOUGH!' came a roar from the shadows as a mighty greataxe thundered down upon the table. Looming over the table and the card players, claws still wrapped around the greataxe, stood a weyre, a wolf beast. White and grey fur, powerful limbs, and fangs and jaws that could tear a foe to pieces. Rough and faded leather armour covered its torso. The beast snorted out its long snout and black nose, growling as its piercing blue eyes peered at the dwarf.

'My friend Fenrix here disagrees with your protest,' Quinlan said as the weyre continued to growl.

'I... I may have been mistaken,' the dwarf said, face pale with fright. 'Take the coins.'

'Good choice,' Fenrix snarled as the dwarf hopped from his seat and hurried away towards the bar.

'Good to see you're both staying out of trouble,' Wraith greeted them. 'Were you cheating?'

'Of course not,' Quinlan replied as he lifted his hand

from beneath the table. He held a light-crossbow, armed with bolt, ready in case needed for the dwarf. Tucked between his fingers were two cards, royal and high scoring.

Fenrix, his greataxe still lodged in the table, walked round and enveloped Wraith in a warm, tight hug.

'You shouldn't have sought out the troll alone,' the weyre said as he released the embrace, 'but I am glad to see you return.'

'You keeping him out of trouble?' she asked, pointing to Quinlan.

'Trying,' the wolf grunted.

'And succeeding, for the most part,' Quinlan said as he flicked a golden coin to Fenrix. 'Are you here to call in my debt to you?'

The debt he spoke of was his attempt, with others, to rob Wraith and Raven on the road to Stonemere. When the thieves turned murderous, Quinlan sided with their victims and a debt was sworn to make up for his mistakes.

'We leave soon,' Wraith said. 'If you are both willing to follow.'

'The Forsaken reunited again,' Quinlan cheered. 'I wonder what heroic tale we will have to retell after this new adventure. Tell me, where do we journey to?'

'Our destination is the Karnock Fortress.'

'Never heard of it,' grunted Fenrix.

'I have,' Quinlan said as his smile quickly faded. 'A ruin, haunted and cursed. We walking into another Stonemere?'

'Possibly,' Wraith admitted. 'We will be far from the first to make the attempt. The target is a family relic, lost somewhere in the crypts. We go to the city of Rheins to learn more before heading to the fortress. You both in?'

'Yes,' Fenrix said with a fanged grin.

'Wait, is this the Lockwood Mausoleum contract?' Quinlan questioned.

'That it is,' the Slayer confirmed.

'Then no. Not a chance. Leave me out of this one,' the highborn quickly declined with raised hands. 'I've heard many terrible tales of that hellhole and I have no wish to join its countless victims.'

'Do you want me to throw you to the mercy of that dwarf you conned?' Fenrix asked.

'You wouldn't,' Quinlan said with shock, but the looks on the faces of Wraith and Fenrix showed they would. 'Fine,' the nobleman muttered. 'Count me in, but I'm not happy about it.'

'When are you happy about anything?' Fenrix chuckled.

'I was happy before she walked in.' Quinlan pointed to Wraith. 'With ale in my cup, a girl at my side, and soon a victory with cards.'

'Who's your friend?' Raven asked the highborn as she joined them with wine cup still in hand.

'This is Cassandra,' the brigand said proudly.

'Crystal,' she corrected with shock. 'Cassandra is my sister. You've been with her?'

'Err… no…' Quinlan stammered, earning himself a slap across the face. Crystal grabbed a dozen coins from the table and hurried away out of the inn.

'My mistake,' Quinlan said as he rubbed his reddened cheek and rose from the table, collecting his pack, sheathed rapier, and twin light-crossbows.

'Wraith!' Kiplan called from the bar. 'You have a delivery from Thainin Thunderhorn!'

'Make yourselves ready to leave,' Wraith told the weyre and the highborn.

'Do you think we should send our friend in the citadel a

message?' Raven suggested. 'We could use her help with this one.'

'I'm one step ahead of you.' Wraith pulled a sealed letter from her cloak. 'Kiplan, can you have a messenger take this for me?'

'Anything for a pretty lady.' The barkeep smiled.

'Well, if it isn't the famous Wraith.' A voice called to her that hit a nerve and made her cringe. 'Heading out for more fame and glory?'

Young and handsome, with green eyes and thick brown hair, Marek Rhihart stood at the bar. Marek was Wraith's rival when she was still an apprentice of the Guild. Arrogant did not begin to describe him, for he completed his training, trial, and even his initial contracts without difficulty, and certainly let anyone who would listen know. That ever present grin and his boastful tendencies infuriated Wraith. There was not a person in the world she disliked more.

'Marek,' Wraith greeted him curtly through gritted teeth.

'I hear you've had a bust up with Limso Murnelly,' he said with too much joy in his voice. 'That thieving halfling will talk himself into an early grave one day.'

'One day soon if he tries me again. You on assignment?'

'Between contracts. Had to deal with a band of goblins near Barslowth three days ago. Turned out there was a shaman leading them. It took me and two others to bring him down, though when the battle was over, only I was left standing.'

'More of the reward for you, I guess?' Wraith presumed Marek would be pleased over that, showing no loyalty to those he worked with, or trained with, in the past.

'Something like that,' Marek replied grimly. 'Only just

got back myself, but I hear you're now headed out. Lock-wood Mausoleum, that right?'

'It is,' Wraith confirmed with annoyance.

'Not the contract I would choose. Though only recently returned, it would not take me long to make ready if you have need of assistance?'

'Not from you,' Wraith taunted as she handed over her letter to Kiplan and then vacated the inn without another word.

CHAPTER FIVE
THE ROAD TO RHEINS

The scholar's map was perfect as always, encompassing every road and turn, crossroads, tavern, and village, and any particular areas that should be avoided, such as bogs or easy ambush points. Wraith had come across highway robbers before, Quinlan amongst them, and was glad to evade such a run-in again.

They travelled south from Varnhelm, circling Aranch Forest before turning North-East. They passed Foledo's Fortune Inn and the route through the forest, reminding Wraith of her trial. The slaying of an escaped siren mesmerising and slaughtering travellers proved her worth to the Guild and gained her induction.

Raven, Fenrix, Quinlan, and Wraith at the lead travelled until darkness claimed the road ahead. They made camp not far from the road, Fenrix keen to keep watch whilst the others slept.

'Thank the Gods,' Quinlan murmured as he stretched out his back. 'The nag I've been riding and its cheap saddle were killing me.'

'You're lucky we gave you a mount at all, bandit,' Raven mocked him. 'Where'd all your gold go, anyway?'

'Debts and debtors.' He grimaced before smiling. 'There's always someone with their hands out.'

'And daggers if you don't pay up,' Wraith joked before turning to Fenrix with concern. 'You need to rest too. You've walked the entire journey whilst we rode.'

'I scare off the horses,' he said with a forced smile.

'You kept apace though. We never had to slow.'

'A gift of my curse,' the weyre replied. 'I don't need nearly as much sleep either. You all rest. I'll wake you when needed.'

'Thank you, wolfie,' Raven called to him as she set to work lighting the fire, Quinlan already beginning to doze without helping make camp at all.

'The full moon should help you see if anyone tries to sneak up on us,' Wraith said.

'I see just fine in the dark,' Fenrix said gruffly, 'and it's not a full moon, not yet. A few days short.'

They slept without disturbance, Raven rising early and hunting a breakfast of rabbit for all. She threw her quarry to Quinlan, the highborn unhappy with his task of skinning their meal and barely keeping the contents of his stomach down. By the time the rabbits were cooked, he had lost all appetite and was actually keen to be on the road again.

'Anyone want to trade horses for a while?' Quinlan moaned farther down the road. 'Loyal looks mighty comfortable.'

'Not a chance.' Wraith patted the neck of her stead. 'As his name suggests, he's loyal to me.'

'Don't you dare even look at mine, bandit,' Raven cautioned.

'Even just the saddle would be...' Quinlan began before Fenrix growled loudly in warning.

'Quiet!' Fenrix said, fangs bared.

'What is it?' Wraith and Quinlan asked.

'Wait,' Fenrix said, taking hold of Loyal's bridle and making the steed stop. The weyre sniffed at the air, snout raised and eyes closed.

'I sense it too,' Raven said, eyes wide in alert. 'Smoke.'

'Fires,' Fenrix warned. 'A lot of them.'

Each of them looked to the skies before spotting the rising dark plumes to the north, back the way they had already travelled.

'Carry on and pretend we haven't seen it?' suggested Quinlan.

Wraith checked the Scholar's map, seeing the only nearby settlement in that direction was Princip village.

'What do you think?' Raven asked Wraith.

'Let's go take a look,' she replied. 'They may need aid. Go, but keep your weapons ready.'

'Go!' Wraith ordered, turning Loyal and kicking back to send him galloping back the way they had come. Raven rode beside her, Quinlan lagging behind, but it was Fenrix who led. No longer on his legs, the weyre bound forward on all fours, the wolf-blood taking hold.

At the next crossroads, they turned towards the rising smoke. The path was deserted, no sign of anyone until they neared the village itself. With the buildings visible and the smoke still rising, three men blocked the road. They wore polished plate armour, shining helms and crimson cloaks, shields emblazoned with the symbol of an aflame torch. Fear rose within Wraith the moment she recognised the symbol as that of the Sacred.

'Stop!' the soldiers ordered. 'Stop right there!'

'What's happened here?' Wraith asked. 'Does anyone need aid?'

'The people of this village are receiving all the aid they need,' the lead soldier stated firmly. 'This is the Sacred's business. Nothing to you. Turn around and go back the way you have come.'

'You don't need to tell me twice,' Quinlan replied.

'Agreed,' Raven added, looking at Wraith again. 'We must leave.'

Wraith looked past the soldiers and into the village. The smoke still rose into the sky, but there was no sign of anyone but more soldiers of the Sacred and their crimson cloaks.

Fenrix growled as he faced the soldiers, all three of them standing firm with weapons drawn.

'Leave now, or your fate will be added to those who called this place home,' the lead soldier warned.

'Let's get back to the road,' Wraith said firmly, urging Fenrix to turn away.

'Good choice.' The soldiers sneered and laughed as Wraith and her companions departed. Fenrix growled in anger, but he too walked away.

'You know what that was, don't you,' Quinlan said to them all once they were out of earshot.

'A cleansing,' Raven said. 'A purge.'

'Someone was hiding a potential within the village,' Quinlan finished. 'These people doomed themselves.'

'Men, women, and children…' Raven said in shock.

'Gone,' Fenrix growled.

'How can this be allowed to happen?' Raven said in anger. 'How can King Rothgard allow this to happen in his country, to his people?'

'Our ruler, the just and honourable King Korinthus Rothgard, is like all royalty throughout the Centuros,'

Quinlan remarked in a pompous tone. 'Trapped, with their balls caught in a vice. The Sacred overrule them and show no leniency. More kings and queens have died by the hands of the Sacred than have been taken by sickness, war, and old age combined.'

'Rothgard is powerless,' Fenrix said darkly.

Wraith remained silent but thought to the child she saw in the carriage headed for the Kasterburg Citadel. This village paid the price for hiding one who possessed arcane ability. All those with such skills were expected and ordered to join the Sacred, the cleansing the punishment for defying the order. The fear within Wraith was because she too was a potential. Only Raven of her companions knew this. She felt the ache within her hands flare, her curse, and silently damned the soldiers and their masters.

CHAPTER SIX
THE CITY OF RHEINS

It was already sunset by the time Wraith, Raven, Quinlan, and Fenrix reached their destination. Smaller than Varn-helm, the city of Rheins was known as a trade hub and for its port but little more. Wraith knew there was no Guild presence here, but the young guards at the gates recognised the branding and permitted her entrance.

'You may enter, but not your companions,' the captain of the guard, a stern woman, declared as she approached and shoved her young comrade aside. 'We're not to permit entry to any new arrivals after sundown. You, we can make an exception for, being as you're here on Guild business.'

'They're with me, on Guild business,' Wraith argued.

'Do they carry the brand?' the captain questioned.

'They do not, Captain Trizzan,' the younger guard replied nervously.

'No, they do not,' Wraith admitted, 'but they each carry one of these.' The Slayer held up three gold coins, one for each of her party.

'Double it and the elf and gentleman may pass, but not

that... beast,' Captain Trizzan said once she saw Fenrix up close. 'What in the hells is it?'

'Not dangerous,' Wraith assured.

'I disagree. The beast waits outside our walls.'

'It's fine,' Fenrix said, without anger or contempt. There was a sadness to his eyes and Wraith sensed this was far from the first time the weyre had been shunned.

'Ten gold and my vow that there will be no trouble from us,' Wraith promised.

Captain Trizzan stared back at Wraith and then looked to each of the group, eyes lingering on Fenrix the most.

'What business has the Guild in our city?' she asked.

'Information only. We seek Viscount Lockwood,' Wraith replied, earning a sly smile from the guard captain.

'The Lockwood Mausoleum, I am sure,' she said with a chuckle. 'Very well. I will grant entry to your party, but it will cost you more than you have offered.'

'Why should we pay?' Quinlan asked. 'Viscount Lockwood will not happy being kept waiting.'

'And I care little for the viscount's happiness,' Trizzan said. 'You are free to wait outside the city until morning.'

'No,' Wraith conceded. 'What cost did you have in mind?'

'Twenty gold for entry.'

Quinlan and Raven winced at the figure.

'Twelve,' Raven offered.

'Twenty,' Trizzan replied firmly.

'Fifteen.'

'Twenty.'

'Eighteen?' Quinlan tried.

'Twenty,' Trizzan said one last time before Wraith shoved the coins into the captain's hand. 'Pleasure to do business with you.' The captain secured away the coins. 'A warning for all of you, no weapons in hand within our city.

You draw a blade in Rheins, you draw the noose. No weapons.'

'Understood.' Wraith nodded as the guards parted way and allowed the group to pass.

'This had better be worth it,' Quinlan muttered as they entered the city and the gates were secured behind them.

'For once, I agree,' Raven said, earning a smile from the brigand.

'Seems we are here for the night and likely closely watched,' Wraith said. 'Stay close and, please, no trouble.'

'You heard our esteemed leader,' agreed Quinlan.

'That goes double for you,' Wraith said.

'Wouldn't dream of it,' he replied innocently, but his eyes were already taking in the city and its opportunities.

Beyond the gates was the city; houses and homes, markets and businesses, guardhouses and a keep, and, of course, an inn or two. Immediately around them were a dozen wagons, newly arrived in the city and needing organisation. A group of children played nearby, two daring to approach Fenrix. The weyre growled at them both, scaring them away and making Quinlan and Raven laugh.

'Were any of you listening to me?' Wraith asked.

'What?' Fenrix grunted innocently.

'Stay close and out of trouble,' Wraith repeated. 'We are here to speak with Viscount Lockwood, and then we are back on the road for Karnock at first light. We don't want any distractions…'

'What is this?' a voice called out from amidst the wagons. 'If it isn't my old acquaintance and saviour.'

'Shit,' Wraith muttered.

Across the courtyard marched a jovial face with a wide smile, short stubby nose, grey hair. The man wore fine clothes. Jefford Hencaster, owner of the Hencaster Emporium.

'My dear, it gladdens the heart to see you again,' Jefford greeted as he bowed and placed a gentle kiss upon Wraith's hand. 'Every day I think of the young girl who saved me from the clutches of that murderous siren. Tell me, are you well?'

'I am,' Wraith said, unable to conceal a smile at the greeting and the looks of surprise from her companions.

'And I see you do not travel alone this time. An elf with eternal beauty, a beast of a wolf, and… wait… I know you. You're Gideon Clively the twelfth or some rubbish like that.'

'Quinlan Vespasian Clysley the Fourth,' the highborn corrected. 'Mr Hencaster, it is good to see you once again. How goes…'

'Wait, I remember now.' Jefford pulled a notebook from his pocket. 'Yes, I never forget a debt. You owe me a hundred and thirty-seven gold pieces due to failure of payment.'

'There's a surprise.' Raven teased. 'Gambling again.'

'My wins outnumber my losses… sometimes,' Quinlan admitted miserably. 'I have not forgotten the debt owed, and it is employment that has brought me to your fair city.'

'Hmm… normally I would set my strongest and roughest men out to collect on a debt of such a long time,' Jefford replied, 'but as you are in the company of my saviour, I will extend the debt for a period. Do not forget.'

'Trust me, *we* won't forget,' Wraith assured. 'How goes business?'

'Better, but always busy, as you can see by the sorry state of this caravan of goods,' Jefford said. 'Demand remains high, supply tight, and coin aplenty if you know where to find it. In fact, the cargo from these wagons is all bound for ships that will take them across the ocean to Kallensia, where they will fetch a pretty penny or two if their captains can evade the pirates that plague our waters.'

'And your brother?' she asked.

'Tybalt no longer holds any control or power within the Hencaster Emporium,' Jefford explained with distaste. 'His dealings with the siren were just the peak of the mountain. He hadn't paid our taxes to the crown for near three years, pocketing the coin! We're lucky the crown didn't take our heads! I am still uncovering more of his illegal actions, and he remains under close watch. Anyway, enough of my sorry brother. What of you? What brings you to Rheins?'

'We seek an audience with Viscount Lockwood,' Wraith explained, earning an outburst of laughter from the merchant.

'Christoph Lockwood, the *viscount*, won't see you now. Not tonight, at any rate,' Jefford said.

'That was twenty gold well spent,' Raven commented.

'What could you possibly want with the viscount?' Jefford asked. 'He's a... serious sort and not to be trifled with if you can help it.'

'We seek information regarding a contract he has taken,' Wraith replied, lifting the sleeve of her armour to reveal the Guild branding.

'My saviour is actually a slayer,' Jefford said with a wide smile. 'I am not surprised, and I am glad that, in this task, I can aid you.'

'For a cost,' Quinlan chimed in.

'No cost,' the merchant replied. 'Not this time. The viscount has been out of the city hunting all day. He will be feasting tonight and in no mood for business. Tomorrow may be possible, early before he begins his usual routine of strangling the livelihood from all merchants within the city with his taxes, myself included. Normally, it would cost you for an audience, but I owe you at least this favour. I will secure you the meeting and send word to you of the place and time. I warn you though, expect a frosty reception. The viscount is not the most patient or welcoming of people.'

'He holds the power in the city?' Wraith questioned.

'The viscount certainly believes so.' Jefford smirked. 'Though he does not hold the backing of his own family to support such an endeavour. Perhaps that is why you seek him out, I wonder.'

'Perhaps. So, we must wait until morning. Can you recommend anywhere we can stay for the night?'

'The city holds many reputable taverns you can seek shelter, a meal, and a bed for the night. The Woodman, The Longe Arms, The Maid's Head. All of these I can recommend, though be warned, the harbour is packed tight with ships this evening. Many crews, despised pirates among them, will seek a night on dry land and an opportunity to spend whatever coin they have. Steer away from The Pale Mere, as I have heard that place attracts rogues, ruffians, and trouble... although, by appearance, that may suit you. My messenger will find you wherever you end up.'

'Thank you, Jefford,' Wraith said.

'It is I who remains eternally thankful of you,' the merchant said gratefully. 'If not for you, I would still be the puppet of the monstrous Siren of Aranch Forest.'

A commotion and crashing of boxes sounded from amongst the wagons, snapping Jefford's attention back to his work.

'I have much to do and the hour grows late,' the merchant said. 'Apologies, but I must depart and take charge of this mess if we are ever going to rendezvous with the ships. Rothgard's taxes on goods strangle us, so this little lot is bound for across the waves to Kallensia. I will seek you out if I have time, but if not, it was an honour and a pleasure to see you again, my dear.'

He bowed, kissed Wraith's hand again, and then quickly marched back to the wagons, yelling orders and barking commands.

'Interesting company you've been keeping,' Raven teased.

'Lucky for us,' Wraith replied. 'Thanks to him, we will have a meeting with the viscount.'

'Not lucky at all,' Quinlan said sadly. 'I'd hoped he'd forgotten I owed him money!'

CHAPTER SEVEN
PALE MERE INN

THE CITY OF RHEINS

'You three, yes. That one, no,' Ballos, the miserable, balding, frail and exhausted innkeeper ordered. He leant heavily on a walking stick but used the bar for support so he could wave the stick at Fenrix. 'We have enough trouble here without inviting... whatever the hell he is inside.'

'Can you really afford to be so picky?' Quinlan asked. 'It's not exactly heaving in here.'

The highborn was right, for the inn was quiet, with only a handful of despondent patrons quietly sipping from their tankards. There were no bards or music, no laughter or joy, and apart from the three gnomish card players in a corner, little conversation. The walls were marked and faded, furnishings in need of repair or worse. Signs of scuffles and fighting were everywhere, blood even marking one of the walls. Apart from the innkeeper, there was a single young serving girl, though even the pair of them seemed more than the required staff for the amount of custom.

'Look, I know why you're here,' Ballos said despondently. 'The other inns are full to the brim so you had no other choice. Well, it's just me and my granddaughter Lucey here. We have beds, and Lucey can cook a decent soup if you're hungry. We've got plenty of ale if you've the coin. You're all welcome, but the wolf stays outside. We have trouble enough bringing in customers.'

Wraith meant to argue or offer coin again as she did at the gates to the city.

'It's fine,' the weyre surrendered. 'It's far from the first time. May I stay in the stables?'

'As long as you don't eat the horses,' Ballos said.

'Depends how good the girl's soup is.' Fenrix chuckled, though the innkeeper's look of warning showed he did not get the joke.

'I'm sorry,' Wraith said as the weyre walked out.

'There's nothing for you to apologise for,' Fenrix reassured before he was gone.

'Now that business is resolved, will it be beds and meals for the night?' Ballos asked.

'And ales,' Raven added as she and Wraith took seats at a nearby table. 'Let's have a drink. It's been a long ride, and already one of my wine bottles from the Coin is empty.'

'You saving the other for the mausoleum?' Wraith asked.

'Absolutely.'

'I see a card game,' Quinlan said merrily.

'Only with your own coin and belongings,' Wraith ordered.

'No promises,' the noble said before joining the card players.

'And how can I help you today?' Lucey, the lone serving girl, asked. She was young, a few years younger than Wraith, with short blonde hair, a pretty smile, and green eyes. *She will break many hearts when she is older,* Wraith thought. *If she escapes this place.*

'Four ales,' Wraith requested. 'Make it five and take one over to our friend at the cards table.'

'Will do,' Lucey replied, looking at Quinlan with a smile before approaching the bar to pour the drinks.

'Should we warn her about our bandit friend?' Raven joked.

'He's harmless,' Wraith replied. 'Most of the time.'

'You think Fenrix is really all right being stuck in the stables?' Raven asked.

'I'll take two of the ales out and check on him. We can work on Ballos until he lets our furred friend inside.'

'Here you go.' Lucey placed the tankards of ale at their table.

'This place ever get busy?' Wraith asked as she took a sip from her tankard. It was good. Warm, but tasted just fine.

'There are a few ships docking tonight,' the barmaid replied, her smile faltering as she spoke. 'Crews often find their way here, for better or worse.'

'You expecting trouble?' Raven asked, but Lucey did not reply.

'Enjoy,' she simply said, leaving four tankards at the table before carrying the last one over towards Quinlan at the card table.

'Might be a more interesting night than expected.' Wraith raised her tankard towards Raven.

'Cheers to that,' the elf replied, clashing their tankards before both drank deep.

'Still not looking forward to entering the mausoleum?' Wraith asked.

'Dreading it.' The elf wiped her chin clean of a dribble of ale. 'But I'll be there when needed, as will the other two.'

'I'm sure of it. I do have one question for you though.'

'Go on,' Raven urged. 'As long as it has nothing to do with crypts or venturing underground.'

'Do you miss being the bodyguard? Working for Guild-master Brevik, I mean.'

'Elements of it,' Raven said with a half contained smile. 'Not the work, but the company.'

'Really?' Wraith asked with surprise.

'It's not what you think. Not like that, anyway,' Raven said, then speaking quietly so they were not overheard, she added. 'Your uncle, he found me when I was still...' She placed a hand to the burnt tip of an ear, her marking of slavery. 'He purchased me and then freed me. I owe him for that and so much more, just as Fenrix owes you. For many years, Brevik and I travelled side by side, but...'

'Boredom set in?' Wraith guessed.

'Something like that. My assignment with you opened my eyes to the wider world and I wanted to see more.'

'Despite the dangers?'

'The dangers and risks are all part of it. I felt more alive facing the horrors of Stonemere than I have in ten years at your uncle's side. Besides, as I protect you, I am still repaying my debt to Brevik.'

'I don't need a bodyguard,' Wraith said for the hundredth time.

'Oh, I know that,' Raven replied with a smirk. 'Not when you can roast your enemies alive.'

'I have no idea what you mean,' Wraith joked, raising a finger to her lips to hush the elf. She rose to stand, lifting the two untouched tankards of ale from the table.

'For wolfie?'

'Don't drink my ale,' Wraith warned.

'No promises.' Raven looked over to Quinlan. 'I'll keep

an eye on our bandit and make sure he doesn't gamble away everything he, and we, own.'

Wraith vacated the inn with tankards of ale in hand and found Fenrix in the stables. The weyre was tending to their horses, feeding them, and brushing them down.

'They're fine as long as I don't try to ride them,' Fenrix said, smelling the air and recognising Wraith's approaching scent.

'Or try to eat them,' she said, handing over the tankards.

'Thank you,' the wolf replied, draining the first tankard in one go.

'I will speak with Ballos again and get you a room.'

'Don't waste your breath. I have had this reaction ever since I was... this.'

'And just how long has that been?' the slayer asked as she took a seat on a nearby bench. 'I don't mean to pry, and you don't need to answer. We just haven't had a chance to talk since Stonemere.'

Fenrix sighed heavily, his powerful shoulders rising and falling. He kept his attention on the horses, brushing down Raven's white charger. 'I'm not from Castille. Not originally. My home lies across the waters, in a kingdom I shall not name. I was not always the wolf. I was human, and I was... happy. My family had wealth and power and my life was set with glories in reach.'

'I sense an *until* coming up,' Wraith said.

'Until I met her,' Fenrix struggled to say. 'I misjudged the wrong person, and this was my punishment. My curse.'

'Appearances can be deceiving.' Wraith rubbed the joints of her hands. 'Is there a cure or a way to break the curse?'

'Not that I have discovered. It will be three years this summer since I became the wolf. I fled my home, my family and people, and have travelled alone ever since. You, the elf, and the gambler are the first to travel with me.'

'We are honoured,' Wraith said with a smile.

'You shouldn't be. I've already cost you gold and misfortune. Be careful my curse does not rub off on you too.'

'Believe me, I have my fair share of curse already.'

As they spoke, a crowd of six approached the inn, loud and raucous, a crew from one of the docked ships. Walking like men, but with green and scaled skin, clawed hands, barbed tongues, and parietal amber eyes, they were reptilians, lizard-kind. They cheered and joked, swore and shoved as they made their way inside, shouting for ale, food, and company.

'You should go inside,' Fenrix urged. 'Raven and Quinlan might need you.'

'Want me to bring you any food?'

'No, the horses will make do,' the wolf joked. 'Keep the ale coming though, would you?'

'Of course. I will keep working on getting you a room inside.'

'Thank you, but there's no need,' he said before a loud crash sounded from within the inn. 'Go. Sounds like you're needed.'

Wraith re-entered the busier inn and heard Ballos's voice over the ruckus. Instantly, she felt her hands ache in warning.

'I warn you all after the mess you made last time,' the innkeeper shouted. 'Remember the city rule; draw a blade, you draw the noose.'

'No need for bladesss, right men?' a reptilian with a patch over one eye called, followed by the cheers of his men. The crew hissed and snapped at each other in their own language before demanding ales and food from the innkeeper and his granddaughter.

'All right, new money,' Quinlan cheered as he approached the crew. 'I've taken these gnomes for all the coin they carry, now it's your turn. Who fancies a card challenge?'

The brigand's offer was met with laughter and jeers, before the nearest reptile knocked aside Quinlan with his long, muscular tail. The nobleman stumbled back, colliding with a table and falling to the floor, cards scattering everywhere. The crew laughed again.

'Hey!' Raven and Wraith yelled as they hurried to Quinlan's side.

'There's no need for that,' Wraith warned the reptilian who struck. The amber eyes narrowed, and it hissed at her before laughing again.

'Lorassh, please,' Ballos pleaded. 'Do not let this be like the last time your crew were here. I have only just got the place looking passable again.'

'Not our fault if you keep wretched company,' the reptile with the eye-patch, the crew's captain, sneered. 'My men have been at sssea for ssseven weeksss and we expect food, drink, and company. Your granddaughter will be a ssstart. Where is ssshe?'

Wraith did not turn to look, but knew the girl was hiding back where the card table was, as were the gnome card players. She shifted to stand in the way, as did Raven, but it was Quinlan who acted first.

'Fine sirs,' he called out as he rose to stand and wiped the blood from his lip. 'You are here to feast and to be entertained. As our fine innkeeper sees to your first need, perhaps I can see to your second by retelling the tale of the Scourge of Stonemere?'

The reptiles spoke amongst themselves with hisses and snaps before Lorassh spoke for them.

'Go ahead, bard,' he encouraged with a flick of his barbed tongue and a cruel grin as his claws tapped impatiently upon the bar.

'I am no bard, but I can spin a yarn as good as any,' Quinlan said before launching into his retelling of their adventure in the doomed village of Stonemere.

The highborn spoke of their arrival on a mission to rescue a mage and apprentice of the Sacred order. In gory detail, he retold of the horrors of Lord Blackthorn's monstrous abominations. Finally, Quinlan relished in retelling of their glorious victory and Wraith's emergence as the scourge of Stonemere, slaying the demons that had taken the village. Once his tale was complete, Quinlan took a bow and expected the reverence and applause he usually received, but this time no praise came, nor a single clap.

'Wasss that true?' hissed one of the lizard crew.

'Every word,' Quinlan swore.

'Horsssessshit!' Lorrassh spat, his crew laughing and jeering.

Quinlan ducked as a goblet was thrown, but he could not evade the second that crashed into a wall close by and showered him with its contents of ale. Angered, he paced towards the nearest reptile, hand upon the hilt of his rapier sword.

'Yessss?' the sailor hissed with cruel delight.

'No blades!' Ballos cried from behind the bar where he cowered.

The reptile Quinlan faced sneered before shoving the highborn hard in the chest, letting its claws tear the highborn's jacket and waistcoat beneath.

'You will pay for that,' Quinlan said indignantly.

'There ssshe isss!' shouted another of the crew as he approached the cards table. 'There'sss our little Lucccey!'

Wraith stepped into the lizard-man's path, blocking the way to the innkeeper's granddaughter.

'Move assside!' the sailor sneered.

'What are you going to do?' the reptile facing Quinlan taunted. 'Nothing, that'sss what.'

'Not nothing.' Raven cut between the pair, and with a swing of her fist, punched the reptile across the face. He staggered back for a moment before turning and smiling.

'That was a missstake, little elf girl,' the sailor warned. 'I'll make you pay!'

'No, you won't!' Quinlan yelled as he brought his fist up under the lizard-man's chin, sending the thug tumbling back in a daze and colliding with his crewmates.

'Now you've done it!' hissed Lorrassh with a flick of his barbed tongue. 'No bladesss, boysss! Teach them that thisss isss our inn!'

Ballos threw himself behind the bar, hiding and crying out for peace as his livelihood was turned into a battlefield. Tables were knocked aside, chairs thrown or used as weapons along with fists, booted kicks, and tackles. Wraith, Raven, and Quinlan were outnumbered two-to-one, but they were making a fight of it against the reptiles. No weapons were drawn, but the fight was vicious enough without them.

Raven leapt between foes, evading fists before striking with her own. Her elvish agility had not been hindered by the ale she had consumed, and she moved with speed and dexterity before leaping onto the back of one lizard-man with arms around his neck, choking. The reptile threw himself backwards, slamming the elf into a wall, but she continued to hold on tight, forcing the sailor to his knees.

Quinlan found his way to the cards table, Lucey and the

gnomes hiding behind him as he swung a tankard and it collided with the temple of a reptilian. The lizard-man hissed with laughter, unfazed by the strike, and slowly paced towards the highborn with sharpened claws ready to kill. Quinlan reached for his rapier but remembered the many warnings of blades and nooses. With his foe looming, he searched for a weapon, finding only a broken and barely standing cabinet nearby. It took little effort to make the cabinet fall and crash onto the reptile, but it didn't slow his adversary for long, as the lizard pulled himself through the debris of broken wood.

Diving across a table, Wraith kicked one reptile hard then barged another out of the way. A stool flew through the air and caught her in the chest, sending her crashing back through another table. As she rose to her feet, it was Lorrassh who faced her, the reptile leader striking and cutting across her cheek, close to her prominent scar. Wraith evaded the sailor's tail as it swung round and crashed down before his claws pinned her against a wall.

'You shouldn't have come here!' the captain warned.

'We were here first,' Wraith said, 'and we didn't come alone.'

A shadow loomed over Lorrassh before an ear-splitting howl deafened all. The sailors recoiled and cowered, but their captain was already within the grasp of Fenrix. The weyre lifted the one-eyed sailor over his head and threw him through the nearest window, smashing through wood and glass. Lorrassh's crew looked on in horror as the towering wolf turned on them, growling menacingly.

'Get out!' Fenrix roared, but the sailors stood still with sudden fear.

The weyre paced towards the nearest who threw a fist at him, but it was the wolf who struck first. Fenrix's clawed fist struck like a hammer and dazed the reptile. The weyre then took hold of the sailor's throat and threw the ruffian across the inn, crashing into one of his crewmates with a sickening thud.

'GET OUT!' Fenrix roared again, and this time the lizard-men did not need further encouragement. They ran, dragging their fallen crewmates with them.

Wraith, Raven, Quinlan, and Fenrix dusted themselves off, picked up a fallen table, and then found what chairs had survived. They each took a seat, and from a broken jug, poured ale into four dented and cracked goblets and tankards. Then, as one, all four of them burst into laughter.

'About time you turned up,' Wraith said to Fenrix as he drained his half-empty goblet.

'Didn't want to spoil your fun,' the wolf replied with a grin.

'Ballos, you still there?' the slayer called out.

'My inn,' Ballos replied in horror as he rose from his hiding place. 'It's as bad as last time.'

'Their captain pays for the damages.' Wraith lifted Lorrassh's coin purse to view and threw it to the innkeeper.

'How?' Raven asked.

'Fast hands. He was too busy with our mighty wolf to notice.'

'My dear,' Quinlan called to Lucey. 'Are you harmed?'

'Not at all, thanks to you.' She smiled.

'Anything for a damsel,' Raven mocked and nudged him.

'A little young for me,' the highborn replied before rubbing his jaw and a rapidly surfacing bruise. 'You have anything stronger?'

'I'm sure we can find a bottle of something somewhere.' Ballos cheered as he realised his problem, Lorrassh and his crew, was gone. 'Thank you for ridding us of them. We will fetch food, drinks, and prepare beds for you. All of you. Four not three.'

Fenrix met the innkeeper's gaze and nodded in appreciation.

'That was a helluva hit you gave that reptile,' Raven said, a rare compliment to Quinlan.

'Yep. That's going to hurt soon,' he replied, looking at his rapidly bruising knuckles.

'I think Lorrassh will be hurting more.' Wraith looked to the smashed windows. 'That glass is thick.'

'So was his skull.' Fenrix laughed heartily. 'Did you hear the noise he made when I picked him up?'

'Sounded like he was going to retch.' Raven laughed. 'As did the others when they saw you, wolfie. Retch and piss themselves!'

Fenrix leant back and unleashed another howl to the cheers of his companions.

CHAPTER EIGHT
LOCKWOOD ESTATE

CITY OF RHEINS

With some aches from the fight and merriment of the night before, Wraith awoke early to news of Jefford Hencaster's success. A meeting with Viscount Christoph Lockwood had been arranged for that very morning at the Lockwood Estate in the heart of the city. The messenger apologised for taking so long to find them, believing the Pale Mare Inn to be the last place they would choose to spend the night.

Wraith found that Fenrix and Raven had already left their beds, but she had to wake the snoring Quinlan with a jug of what she thought was water. She left the highborn to wash himself down again properly, heading downstairs and finding Fenrix devouring his second plateful of breakfast. Breads, beans, and porridge was provided; simple but filling. Wraith savoured her share too before approaching the innkeeper for payment. Ballos had cut the fee in half as thanks for their actions the previous night, and Wraith was pleased and surprised to find Raven had already paid what was due.

She found the elf in the courtyard beside the stables, bow in hand and quiver of arrows at her back. Across the yard from her was a target, a dozen arrows already lodged in a wide pattern. Wraith had retrieved the bow from the ruins of Stonemere, and upon discovering the elvish markings along its length, knew it had to be returned to its people, Raven the only candidate. Since then, the she-elf had practiced each morning, rising at first light.

'Good morning,' Wraith greeted. 'How's the practice coming along?'

'Slow,' the she-elf replied. 'There was a time when I was still amongst my people that I could hit a target dead-centre every time, no matter the range. It will take time and practice to return to anything close to that again.'

'You're better than many I've seen. Have you thought of one day seeking out your people? With your newfound freedom, I am certain we could make a journey that would…'

'Stop.' Raven lowered her bow. 'Do not speak of what you do not know and do not understand. I cannot go back and that is all we shall speak of it.'

'I am sorry. I shouldn't have pried.'

'No. I'm sorry,' Raven said with regret. 'We will talk of this another day, but not now. Not with what we have ahead of us.'

'Conversing with nobility and then descending into a haunted tomb,' Quinlan greeted merrily as he and Fenrix approached. 'It is just another day for the heroes of the Forsaken!'

'You smell dreadful,' Raven said.

'Yeah, he does.' Fenrix grinned.

'Thank our beloved leader for that,' the brigand muttered. 'To the Lockwood's?'

'To the Lockwood's,' Wraith confirmed.

They left their horses at the Pale Mere stables and made the short walk across the city to the Lockwood Estate, following innkeeper Ballos's directions. What awaited them was a grand three-storey building with iron gates surrounding the grounds and gardens. From flag poles flew the red griffin of Castille, along with the coat of arms of a sword raised in an armoured fist. There were guards at the gates who eyed the approaching group of four with suspicion, especially Fenrix. Not far from the guards hung a rotting skeleton from the top of the gates, ravens pecking at the remaining flesh. Its hands had been removed, and across the forehead of the skull the word THIEF was carved.

'What business have you at Lockwood Estate?' asked the guard as Wraith and her companions approached. His armour was marked with the same coat of arms as appeared on the flag above.

'We have a meeting this morning with Viscount Lockwood,' Wraith announced.

The guard checked his listing, smirking before looking to the group.

'I have instructions to be expecting a young Slayer of the Guild,' the guard said. 'A she-elf, a wolf, and a swindler.'

'That would be me,' Quinlan said with wounded pride.

'You three are permitted entrance, leaving all weaponry here,' the guard replied, prompting the arrivals to disarm begrudgingly. 'Not the… wolf. He stays here too.'

'No surprise there,' murmured Fenrix, before eyeing the nervous guards with a sly grin. 'I will wait and keep these fine fellows company.'

Wraith meant to argue but realised this was different to

the city gates and the inn. They needed the information the viscount possessed.

'We will not be long,' she promised.

'I will keep an ear out for trouble.' Fenrix winked.

Wraith, Raven, and Quinlan were escorted across the estate's courtyard and then inside. They were greeted by the smell of wood, oil, and wine. Upon every table and cabinet and at every window were vases of beautiful fresh flowers. Distinguished portraits and finely crafted tapestries hung upon the walls, and stone statues and busts lined the corridors. Quinlan, distracted by the fine wealth on display, tripped on the carpet and stumbled into one of the pillars, sending the stone bust of a nobleman over a hundred years old tumbling to the ground. Raven reacted quickly, grabbing the bust and placing it safely atop the pillar again as her highborn companion apologised and cautiously backed away.

There was a commotion of raised voices and arguments coming from many of the rooms they passed as they were led up the staircases to the highest floor. Any nearby servants gave a low bow, and Wraith was not alone in spotting the burnt tips of elven ears among them. She shared a look with Raven, sensing her anger, and took her hand, squeezing tight in support.

Upon arrival at the viscount's study, the guard knocked at the oak door and waited for a response. After a long pause, a voice finally answered.

'Enter,' called a distinguished tone.

The guard opened the door and entered, Wraith, Raven, and Quinlan following, with another guard close behind. Curtains were drawn, the light provided by candles upon the desk where a beautiful and clearly highborn elven woman sat. Books, parchments, and letters covered the desk, along with a dagger that was embedded in the wood. At a hearth with a raging fire stood a man, hair receding and square jaw, with age lines around his eyes. He tossed papers into the flames and wore a nobleman's shirt and jacket, with a slender rapier similar to Quinlan's sheathed at his hip. Wraith, Raven, and Quinlan were shown to seats with the guards standing close behind, ever watchful.

'It is not easy to secure an audience at such short notice,' the man at the hearth commented as he threw the last of the papers into the flames. 'Even with the favour and support of Jefford Hencaster.'

'And coin,' commented the elven noblewoman as she looked through the letters at the desk, caring nothing for their arrivals.

'This is my wife, Lady Aureilia Lockwood,' the man, clearly Viscount Christoph Lockwood, said. 'I was intrigued by the description of your party. A Slayer of the Guild, a wolf, a swindler, and a she-elf.'

'She-elf,' Lady Lockwood commented, finally looking up and peering close. 'Tell me of your lineage. What family dynasty do you originate? Where do you call home?'

'I... I...' Raven stammered, surprised by the sudden questioning before the noblewoman stopped her.

'Wait,' she said dismissively with a disgusted gaze. 'I see your branding. You are nothing but a slave. Do not speak in our presence for you are not fit.'

'Raven is no slave,' Wraith protested as both Raven and Quinlan were shocked silent by the sudden outburst. 'Do not speak to her like that.'

'You will not speak to my wife in such a way,' the viscount ordered with a face of thunder.

'Apologies,' Wraith said with bowed head. 'I meant no offence.'

Wraith risked a glance to Raven and was surprised that

instead of the anger and rage she expected, she saw fear and disgrace.

'Offence has been taken,' Lady Aureilia protested.

'I should have mind to toss the lot of you out of my home this instant,' Viscount Lockwood stated coldly. 'Or worse, clapped in irons and dragged to a cell. Who are you to speak in such a manner?'

'The Forsaken,' Wraith said, attempting to hold her nerve and sound confident.

'Am I meant to be impressed? Am I meant to know what or who that is? I have never heard of you, and in your line of work, that is not a good thing.'

'Regardless, you have need for people in our line of work,' Quinlan said. The change in the viscount's face confirmed Quinlan was right.

'Yes,' he admitted with a heavy, frustrated sigh.

Lady Lockwood rose from her seat and stormed across the study. At the door, she stopped and turned back, looking at Raven with disgust.

'Not that I believe for one second you will be successful,' she sneered, 'but if you do find anything else of worth bearing the Lockwood seal, bring it to us. We will see you rewarded... and it certainly looks like you could use the coin.' Lady Lockwood then turned to her husband. 'I will return when you have more worthy company.'

With that, she left, slamming the door behind. In the wake of his wife, the viscount crossed the room to his desk and picked up a single letter.

'Hencaster informed me you are here with questions regarding my contract?' Lockwood said. 'I must say, I am far from impressed by your Guild's attempts so far.'

'We are here to rectify that,' Wraith said with as much certainty as she could muster in the face of the noble.

'Thank you for granting us this time. We have questions but will make them brief.'

'You had better,' the viscount warned, with cold eyes and a raised brow.

'Tell us of Karnock.'

Lockwood drew their attention to the large painting framed and hung upon the wall behind the desk. The painting displayed a vast castle, Karnock in its former glory. Tall towers, high battlements, a courtyard filled with people and animals, knights, and merchants, and a vast keep at its heart.

'My family was one of the first noble houses in Castille,' the viscount explained. 'My ancestors fought in the Dark Days against the corrupt and malevolent sorcerers that waged war across our lands. Karnock was the site of one of the fiercest battles lasting ten days before the foulest of the arcane sorcerers known as Zarakahn was cast down. It was a Lockwood who dealt the killing blow, and Karnock was our reward. Our mighty fortress was our seat of power in the realm, guarding the passes through the Sky Peak Mountains to the North-East. The Lockwoods were revered and praised by rulers, kings and queens often in attendance for lavish feasts and celebrations.'

'What happened?' Wraith asked. 'From what I hear, Karnock looks nothing like that now.'

'Rumour has it the fortress had a run in with arcane masters again,' Quinlan said with caution.

'For once, rumour was right,' Lockwood said angrily. 'Karnock, the home of my ancestors, was purged by the Sacred. The cause and reasons were lost with the dead within that fortress, but my great, great grandfather escaped the cleansing. Some sought revenge for the destruction of near my entire noble house, but they too were lost. Vengeance against the Sacred is not possible and not something I seek.'

'What you seek is within the ruined fortress,' Wraith said. 'Tell us of the mausoleum.'

'The Lockwood family vault,' the viscount corrected. 'Buried deep beneath Karnock, it was excavated and cleared once my descendants were awarded the fortress. From that day until the cleansing, my ancestors were interred within the crypts. Every member of my family was entombed alongside their prized possessions; tokens of family, love, and honour.'

'How big is the family vault?'

'I will not lie to you, it is vast. There are four entrances, and at least two known levels beneath the ground of the fortress. What remains though, I cannot be certain, for much of the fortress and its keep have collapsed over time. The foundations and the family vault are likely as ruined as the fortress above.'

'And its defences?' Raven asked, still shaken by Lady Lockwood's scorn but trying to focus on the viscount's instructions.

'I am afraid those details were lost with the fortress,' Lockwood admitted. 'What I do know is that of the four entrances, it was the northern that was preferred. Why, I could not tell you, but what I seek is among those tombs.'

'You want us to be grave-robbers?' Raven chuckled.

'Surely that's something that is not beneath you?' Lockwood sneered with a glance at the three of them.

'And the relic itself?' Quinlan asked. 'Grave-robbery, I understand, but we know little of what we are to find.'

'A longsword known as the Lockwood Lance,' the viscount said.

'Not confusing at all,' Quinlan whispered under his breath, drawing a silent but needed chuckle from Raven.

'It was the very weapon that slew the dreaded sorcerer Zarakahn,' the viscount explained. 'For centuries it was carried by the head of our family, seen as a standard to rally the Lockwoods and our allies. It was interred with my ancestor, Lord Lavenell Lockwood, within the mausoleum, sealed away and lost.'

'And now you want it,' Wraith said.

'Need it,' he corrected with a hardened gaze. 'I started with nothing, barely two coppers to my name. I have dragged this family back from the gutter, rebuilding from scratch, and now I lead a merchant empire and stand viscount of this city. I have earnt a fortune trading across the realm and have a strange-hold on all goods shipped between Castille and Kallensia across the waves.'

'Slaves?' Raven asked, thinking back to the servants she had seen. Lockwood did not answer, and an uncomfortable silence descended on them.

'If you already have so much wealth and power, what need have you for an ancient sword?' the slayer asked.

'The lance's worth is not as a monetary value, but as a symbol.'

'Explain.'

'There are those within my family, brothers and uncles, who still fight and squabble for control. I am sure you heard them within this very building. They do not believe I am fit to lead and am little more than a merchant. I would prove them wrong and unite my family under one banner; my banner.'

'The Lockwood Lance,' Wraith said. 'Describe it.'

The viscount exhaled with annoyance, his patience rapidly weaning with the continued questions. 'A longsword broken midway down the blade. There is a sapphire gem at the centre of the cross-guard and a jade stone at the pommel. What remains of the sword's blade is marked black, the metal corrupted by the blood of the sorcerer it killed. It is unmistakable by those of my family. As I have already stated, it should be interred in the tomb of Lavenell Lockwood.'

'Do you know where Lavenell's tomb is located within the mausoleum?'

'No.'

'And you're happy with us disturbing the sacred remains of your ancestors?' Quinlan asked with a hint of disgust.

'Lavenell is no longer using the blade, and I have need for it,' Lockwood answered. 'You need not concern yourselves with this, for you have to reach the tomb first. None who have made the attempt have returned.'

'Why do you not seek out the blade yourself?' Raven dared to ask. 'Surely that would convince your family better than hiring others to do your dirty work?'

'My time and my life are too valuable to risk such an endeavour. I have fought for everything you now see around you. Every penny and every brick. I would not lose it all amongst the dead of my ancestors, not now.'

'How many have attempts have already been made on this contract?' Wraith asked.

'Seven that I am aware of, ranging from lone thieves to experienced parties of knights and misguided adventurers. The worst was this lone boy, seeking to make a name for himself. Come to think of it, I'm not sure he had even been inducted into your ridiculous Guild.'

The viscount's words sparked in Wraith's head.

'Do you recall the boy's name?' she asked.

'Lionel… Lumor… Londer…'

'Luthor?' Wraith suggested, barely able to hide her interest and excitement.

'Perhaps,' Lockwood replied dismissively. 'A nervous

and unsure young thing, he was. I am certain he would not have lasted long where so many others perished.'

'Yet you sent him anyway,' Wraith said with a flash of anger that merely drew a cruel smile from the viscount.

'Who is Luthor?' Quinlan asked before Raven elbowed him hard in the ribs.

'Now, enough questions,' the viscount declared as he fixed them each with a cold, hard gaze. 'Based on our *conversation* here, you have left me far from impressed. I do not for one moment believe you are capable of such a task, but if you are somehow successful, then your reward awaits you.'

'Thank you for your time,' Wraith said, nodding to Raven and Quinlan that they were finished. 'We will return with your family blade.'

'Sure you will.' The viscount waved them away as he looked to the papers on his desk. By the time they had reached the door, Lockwood had already forgotten Wraith and her Forsaken companions.

CHAPTER NINE

DERRIEN FORREST

'I do hope you are not taking Lady Lockwood's words to heart,' Quinlan said to Raven. 'She is the worst kind of nobility; cruel, snobbish, and pig-headed.'

'You would know,' Wraith tried to joke, but it had little effect on her elvish companion, whose distant gaze was fixed on the road ahead.

The group had left Rheins and was travelling north through the Derrien Forest. The road and route they took was overgrown and near reclaimed by the forest, requiring some difficult manoeuvring at times for them all to pass. They were still a day's ride from Karnock Fortress and were moving with all the haste they could manage.

'She should never have spoken to you like that,' Quinlan continued.

'I should be used to it by now,' Raven replied. 'It is the same from almost all of my kin I have met since…' Her fingers found the tips of a burnt, pointed ear. 'It's fine. My connection with the elves has not been the same for some time. It is my burden to bear.'

'It shouldn't be,' Fenrix grunted.

'At least being here among the trees should cheer you,' Quinlan suggested. 'Does being amongst nature remind you of home, wherever that is?'

'Sadly not.' Raven sighed heavily. 'My connection with nature is as distant as it is with my kin. I can track well enough, but even that skill is not what it once was. Before I was... taken... I knew those who could learn the history of a tree by touch, see through the eyes of all nearby animals, and control swarms of insects by command. I once could feel the very soul and essence of all life around me. Now, in the midst of this forest, I feel... nothing.'

'I'm sorry, I shouldn't have mentioned it,' Quinlan said sincerely. 'I know what it is to lose everything, but I cannot imagine how tormented you must be by this and by those who should be honoured to see you as kin.'

'Thank you for trying,' Raven said with a slight smile on her lips.

'I did not like the viscount either.'

'We cannot always choose our employers,' Wraith replied.

'Oh, I know that all too well,' the highborn said. 'There was just something about him I did not like. Perhaps it was just nerves and frustration...'

'Your own, you mean?' Wraith asked.

'Yes.'

'We really need to get you a girl, don't we?' Fenrix mocked the former-bandit. 'You've gone too long without one.'

'I cannot argue there,' Quinlan agreed.

'So, Wraith,' Raven said, cheered by Quinlan's kind

words earlier, 'you think it was your old friend Luthor who has come this way?'

'He did set out east from Varnhelm. It's too much of a coincidence for me.'

'Who's Luthor?' Quinlan and Fenrix asked.

Before they could answer, something rustling amongst the trees and bushes came hurtling towards them.

'Stop!' Wraith called out, but the warning was not needed as the horses reared up in fright.

From amongst the bushes stumbled a small creature, tumbling to the road and collapsing in a small bundle. Its furred body rose and fell from breathing, but it did not move more.

'What is it?' Quinlan, the closest, asked as he slipped down from his saddle, stretched out his back, and then approached.

'Careful,' Raven warned.

'It's fine,' Quinlan reassured them as he stood over the animal and leant down to take a close look. 'It's just a...'

A monstrous roar sounded from the sky above the forest before a blur soared down through the branches and landed on the road ahead of them, taller even than those on horseback. The body and head of a mighty lion, wings of a gigantic bat, and tail ending in a cluster of deadly spikes. Its jaw snapped at the riders and the lone standing highborn, displaying rows of sharpened fangs.

'Manticore,' each member of the party said in shock as the beast roared once again. Fenrix gripped his greataxe tight, Raven slowly drew her curved knives, and Wraith reached for Shatter beneath her cloak.

Quinlan recoiled in fear and tripped, falling to the ground. He tried to crawl away but felt something land and crawl up his leg and along his body. It was the small bundle that had fallen into the road, a tiny version of the monster that roared and threatened. A baby manticore.

The adult roared again but did not advance, simply waiting and watching in the middle of the road.

'It's not attacking,' Wraith said, warning the others with a hushed voice. 'It just wants its child back. Don't make any sudden movements, any of you.'

'I'm trying not to move,' Quinlan struggled to say and not startle the young creature upon him. The baby manticore continued to climb his body before nuzzling against his chest, head finding the palm of his hand.

'I think it likes me.' Quinlan laughed, and the adult roared again. The baby lifted its head and looked the highborn in the eye. Its gaze was broken as its parent growled menacingly, the baby leaping away with barbed tail flickering in its wake.

The baby ran to its parent, heads nuzzling for a moment in greeting between parent and child. The adult lifted its offspring onto its back and then looked back to the party, who were still frozen in place. The manticore growled once more, perhaps in acknowledgment or thanks, before a single beat of its wings sent it and the baby on its back into the air. Within moments, the beast and its child were lost from sight.

'Oh my Gods,' Quinlan muttered, head falling back upon the road.

'I cannot believe it.' Wraith laughed with relief. Fenrix was laughing too as he picked Quinlan up and thumped the highborn on the back.

'I thought they were extinct,' Raven said as she looked to Quinlan. 'You all right?'

'Pretty such I need a new pair of breeches.'

'What about your hand?' Wraith asked as she saw the highborn soothe his palm.

'It's nothing. Little rascal cut me as it… as it leapt away.'

The brigand stammered and stumbled for a moment before falling to a knee. Wraith and Raven hurriedly dismounted as Fenrix tried to help him to stand.

'Was it the tail?' Raven asked. 'Was it the tail that cut you?'

Quinlan did not respond. His skin had paled, and his eyes were struggling to remain open and focussed. He swayed and would have fallen if Fenrix had not caught him.

'Manticore tails are poisoned,' Raven warned as she inspected the wound. She lifted the hand to her nose and instantly turned away, sickened and confirming with a nod of her head.

'What do we do?' Fenrix asked with grave concern as Quinlan began to tremor and fit in his arms.

'Waste a vial,' Wraith declared as she pulled from her cloak one of the antidotes she had procured from the Guild's Alchemist. She uncorked the vial and forced its contents into Quinlan's mouth before holding it shut to ensure the liquid was swallowed.

'Will it work?' Raven asked, fearful for the noble.

'No idea, but what other choice do we have?'

As Quinlan continued to shake in his arms, Fenrix closed his eyes and prayed to the Gods.

'Halim, deity of healers and health, save this poor fool. Lords of Loralaye, sisters three, in your home we dwell and ask for your favour. Save him, please.'

His words fell quiet, and for several moments, they all waited in silence until Quinlan ceased to tremor.

'Is he…' Wraith began to ask, fearing the worse.

'Feeling… much… better,' whispered the weak voice of Quinlan.

'You scared us!' Raven yelled at him as Fenrix helped the highborn to stand.

'I scared... myself,' Quinlan barely said, before he swayed and then plummeted towards the ground. This time, Fenrix was not quick enough to catch him.

'He's out cold.' Fenrix grinned as he gently picked up the brigand and threw him over his furred shoulder. 'C'mon, fella. I'll give that nag of yours a break. A manticore, can you believe it?'

'I don't know if it's a good or a bad omen.' Wraith said with disbelief. 'You all right carrying him?'

'He weighs less than my axe.' Fenrix laughed.

'Lead on then.'

Raven seized the reins of Quinlan's horse and led it on, gaze occasionally returning to the highborn on Fenrix's shoulder.

'I did not know you prayed,' Wraith said to the weyre.

'Desperate times,' Fenrix replied. 'As you can likely guess, my relationship with the gods is strained at best.'

'Let's hope they're with us. Where we're going, I think we'll need them.'

Raven pulled her remaining wine bottle from one of the saddlebags, uncorked it, and drank deeply.

CHAPTER TEN

THE RUINED FORTRESS OF KARNOCK

Despite the rigours of time, war, and the cleansing by the Sacred, what remained of the fortress was still impressive and imposing. Much of the foundations of the walls, towers, and other structures still stood, though barely any were half the size of their former glory. Past the gaping holes in the walls, the fallen rubble of buildings could be seen, most prominent of all being the keep. The broken shell of the keep itself had fallen, the stone cracked open and scattered, suffering the worst of the destruction.

With what survived, it was not difficult for Wraith, Raven, Quinlan, and Fenrix to picture Karnock's former glory and what had been home to the formerly honourable Lockwood family.

'So, this is the place where the Lockwood's struck down the dreaded sorcerer Zarakahn?' Raven asked.

'Supposedly so,' Wraith replied.

'Looks they really prospered here,' Quinlan joked as they looked upon the ruins.

'Tracks,' Raven called to her companions as they neared

the outer wall. 'Boots and horses, many of them. Recent too.'

'The viscount said there had been others,' Wraith said.

'But not this recent,' Fenrix stated, his head raised and sniffing the air. 'Elf... human... dwarf... halfling, and gnome. Fiend too and... and...'

'Giant,' Quinlan stammered as he peered through a gap in the wall.

The others saw it too, a pair of them, as tall as four men, lumbering through the ruined fortress. They wore tarnished rags and carried tree trunks as clubs. Guttural grunts served as their language, and the ground tremored around their heavy footsteps.

'Hill giants,' Wraith recalled from her teachings at the Guild as an apprentice. 'Dim-witted brutes, but dangerous if angered or hungry. They must've come down from the Skypeak Mountains.'

'We can just wait for them to pass,' suggested Raven.

'They'll get bored soon enough,' Quinlan agreed.

'Not likely.' Fenrix sniffed the air. 'Horses.'

The weyre was right, as soon, terrified cries of horses sounded from somewhere within the fortress grounds. At the distress of their kin, Wraith, Raven, and Quinlan's own mounts began to pull away and retreat.

'Tie them up,' Fenrix advised as the cry of horses was quickly joined by another's voice.

'HELP! HELP ME! HELP!'

Their own horses were quickly tied to a nearby tree before the four of them clambered through the gaps in the ruined walls and entered the fortress grounds. With weapons drawn, they ran toward the cries for help, recognising them as belonging to a young boy. Beyond the fallen stone of another building, they saw what appeared to be a campsite, twenty tents posted with two fires and near two dozen horses. The giants thundered towards all of it with greed and hunger in their eyes.

One unlucky horse tied to a post could not flee the giant's grasp. The unfortunate gelding was seized and lifted into the air before its terrified screams were silenced as rotten teeth took a bite. Head, neck, and shoulders were torn free, and with a sickening crunch, chewed and then swallowed.

As one giant feasted on the horse, the second loomed over the boy, who still cried for aid. With tears streaming down his terrified face, he faced the enormous scavengers raiding his camp with shaking spear raised. He could have been no more than twelve years old.

'We must save him,' Wraith said as she broke into a sprint. Raven was with her, curved daggers in hand. Quinlan was a little behind, light crossbow drawn but fearful eyes only upon the towering foes. Fenrix raced ahead, bounding on all fours, but all of them were too late as the giant's club came soaring down and crushed the boy from sight in an instant. As one, Wraith, Raven, Quinlan, and Fenrix came to a stop as the giants turned to face the new threat, the four members of the Forsaken. The horse's corpse was tossed aside and club shaken free of the boy's remains.

'Not our best moment,' Quinlan remarked.

'Back the way we came,' Wraith ordered. 'Get ba…'

An arrow whistled through the air and struck straight through the first giant's eye. The lumbering foe staggered and rubbed at the eye, moaning in anger before another arrow soared and struck not far from the second eye. A spear then soared, and then another, the giant forced to shield itself from the bombardment. Wraith and her companions could only watch as, from amongst the rubble of the keep, emerged thirty warriors of all races, charging the giants. Axes, swords, bolts, arrows, and spears assaulted the giants, but still they stood.

Fenrix could hold himself back no longer. The weyre bound forward and leapt at the nearest giant, the one bloodied by its horse victim, as the survivors of the camp fought the brute who killed the boy. Fenrix clawed himself up and onto the giant's back, hacking away with his axe and biting until he was thrown clear.

'Go!' Wraith ordered, forcing herself, Raven, and Quinlan to the aid of their cursed companion.

Quinlan fired bolts from his crossbows, peppering the towering foe, as Wraith and Raven charged closer with shortsword and daggers drawn. Before they could near, the brutal club crashed down in front of them, forcing Wraith to duck away. Raven took her chance, leaping onto the club and running along the giant's outstretched arm. She leapt with daggers ready to strike at her foe's gigantic head. She never reached the target, as the giant swatted the elf away like she was a fly. Raven crashed down amongst the group fighting the second giant, lost amongst the fray.

Wraith snarled, and with hands aching and begging for release, she charged forward. The club swung towards her again, but she ducked, and when near enough, climbed the stone ruins and leapt, Shatter and her silver dagger drawn. Wraith slammed her blades down onto the giant's chest, cutting deep with both weapons, and she prayed she had struck something of importance.

The giant merely looked down and grinned. With ease, the brute reached down and seized the Slayer, lifting her into the air and towards his stinking, bloodstained mouth. With blades torn from her grip, Wraith tried to force herself free, twisting and hitting at the fingers around her. The hold was tight and unforgiving, crushing the air from her lungs and pinning her cloak containing her weapons and vials away from her grasp. Fenrix leapt and struck with his axe again, and Quinlan continued his assault with his crossbows, but the giant was undaunted, Wraith a certain for his next grotesque meal.

A white light, brighter than the sun, blinded all standing in the ruined fortress. A boom like thunder deafened and set ears ringing. Struck blind, deaf, and for a moment dazed and dumb, Wraith felt herself fall and land onto the hard ground below. The fingers of the giant still held her, though the grip had significantly lessened. As her eyesight returned, she saw the giant's arm had been severed just above the wrist, the hand now lying limp and lifeless with Wraith in its palm.

Freed, she looked up and saw a bright, shimmering form. Pale blue skin, long vibrant purple hair, two short black horns at the forehead, extended razor sharp wings, and a dark pointed tail. A fiend descended from the devils of another realm and plane of existence. Crimson robes marked with the aflame torch of the Sacred, she held a spear tipped with three points aloft in the air. Violet eyes shone brightly, flickering with arcane.

'Jaks,' Wraith stammered, earning a smile of fangs from the sorcerer before the fiend's glowing purple eyes turned on the crippled giant clutching its ruined stump. The giant howled in pain as its vast eyes blinked furiously for focus from the fiend's blinding arrival. The second giant, wounded and still surrounded by the other party of warriors, lumbered closer, both behemoths focused on the mage.

'Glad I have your attention,' she declared with pleasure, lifting her spear high before slamming the butt of its staff to the ground. An immense crack of thunder sounded, and a visible blast of power rose and struck both giants, forcing them back a step as they clapped their hands to their ears. Fear overwhelmed both towering foes, and they hurried away, tripping and falling in their haste, destroying more of the ruined stonework in their flight of panic.

The fiend swayed a moment from the effort of the arcane before offering a hand to the still prone Wraith.

'Quite the entrance,' the Slayer said, taking Jaks' hand and rising up to her. Quite by surprise, the fiend enveloped Wraith in a warm, tight hug.

'You do know I have a flair for the dramatic!' Jaks grinned with her fangs showing.

'Sorcerer.' Fenrix nodded as he limped towards them.

'Wolf,' she simply replied, smile unfaltering.

'I never thought I'd be glad to see one of your kind appear,' Quinlan added as he joined them and looked at the severed giant's hand. 'Remind me to never cross you.'

'My dear, Quinlan. I am certain you have sinned enough to lose both hands many times over.'

'Probably,' he agreed sheepishly, dusting down his waistcoat and jacket in an attempt to impress.

'Halt!' a noble, commanding voice called out as a man in full plate armour crossed the courtyard towards them with broadsword raised. Angered grey eyes stared out from beneath a narrowed brow. His shining and polished armour and weaponry, and even his closely trimmed beard, showed no expense had been spared. Upon his shield was the emblem of a sword raised in an armoured fist. The Lockwood coat-of-arms.

'Who are you and why are you here?' the man demanded.

'Helping you, it seems,' Wraith called back. 'And not a moment too soon.'

'We did not need your help,' he spat as several of the group who engaged and blinded the giant joined his side.

'You fail to answer my questions. State who you and your intent, or you too will feel the edge of my blade!'

'Wait, Sir Antonius,' another voice yelled. Sprinting through their group was a golden-haired male adorned in leather armour with a cross belt housing a handful of daggers of various sizes. He moved with graceful agility, and Wraith noticed that through his golden hair were the ruined, burnt tips of elven ears.

'I believe we have a shared goal,' the elf said as he came to stand between Wraith and armoured knight. 'Are you of the Guild?'

'I am,' Wraith said, raising the sleeve of her armour to reveal the branding at her arm.

The elf did similar, revealing the intricate design of a roaring beast, poisoned dagger, silhouette, and locked box forming within a diamond. His poisoned dagger was most prominent, the elf an assassin by trade.

'The diamond,' Wraith stated. 'You're of the Guild in the capital.'

'Yes. Aelthorn be our home, and Aederan Limassehn be my name. Greetings, fellow travellers. And what, pray tell, be your names?'

'Wraith,' she said. 'And we are known as the Forsaken, of the Varnhelm Guild.'

'Wraith, Forsaken, I have heard of those names. You were the ones at Stonemere, weren't you?'

'The scourge of Stonemere,' Quinlan proudly announced as he approached. 'Would you like to hear tell of the already famous tale?'

'Not now,' Wraith said with annoyance as she pushed him away.

'The Varnhelm Guild, huh?' Sir Antonius muttered. 'No doubt hired by my brother Haddrian, or my cousin Christoph, the self-proclaimed viscount of Rheins.'

'And your name?' Wraith asked.

'Sir Antonius Lockwood, rightful heir to the Lockwood family mantle and the true owner of all you see around you.'

Fenrix and Quinlan struggled to stifle their laughter as they looked at the ruins.

'It needs a bit of work,' Jaks taunted.

'How dare you attempt to...'

'How dare you!' Jaks roared back with raised wings and bared fangs. 'I am Jakseyth Sondolar, acolyte of the order of the Sacred! You will show me the respect my order demands!'

Upon the fiend's angered words and seeing the emblem upon her robes, the knight fell to a knee, head bowed in reverence. All around him knelt, all except Raven as she emerged from their number.

'It's good to see you, but I ain't bowing,' the elf remarked as she joined them.

'Nor will I,' Fenrix said sternly, with his arms crossed.

'Neither would I expect you to, my dear,' Jaks greeted warmly. 'You have earned that right, but these... *people* have not.'

'Apologies,' the golden-haired Aederan said as he knelt with his head bowed low. 'I am certain that if my companion, Sir Antonius, had recognised your authority, he would never have spoken out of turn.'

'I await the knight's apology,' the sorcerer replied as she leant on her spear.

'I... am sorry for my rudeness,' Sir Antonius begrudgingly said.

'And?' Jaks encouraged, winking at Wraith and Raven as she indulged in the torture.

'And I vow not to make such a mistake again.'

Jaks knelt down and whispered into Lockwood's ear. 'If

you ever show anything but respect for me, my order, or my companions, I will see to it that you live the rest of your days as the pond scum you just proved yourself to be.'

'Understood.'

'Rise,' Jaks instructed. 'All of you, rise.'

They did so, and as they stood, Wraith could see in full the party of Antonius Lockwood and Aederan Limassehn. There were thirty of them; humans, elves, gnomes, dwarves, a red-skinned and long-horned fiend, a surprisingly large female ogre, and two young boys of a similar age to the boy crushed by the giants. It was quite an assortment, its number easily dwarfing Wraith's.

'What are your orders, my lady?' Antonius Lockwood said to the sorcerer, though there was still more than a hint of resistance in his tone.

'Oh, I do not lead here,' Jaks said, taking a step back and behind Wraith.

'Now we are calmed, we can speak of business,' Wraith stated aloud for all to hear. 'It is clear we are all in pursuit of the same prize, the Lockwood Lance, buried in the mausoleum beneath our feet. Now, am I right in thinking there are no rules within the Guild that say multiple parties cannot compete for the same contract?'

'None,' Aederan agreed.

'And there are multiple entrances to the tombs below?'

'Four,' confirmed Sir Antonius begrudgingly.

'Then I suggest we split the entrances between us,' Wraith said. 'Two each. First to the prize completes the contract, uncontested between our groups.'

'A race to the prize,' Aederan said, with bright eyes. 'I like a challenge. We should place bets.'

'As first here, we take the pick of entrances,' Lockwood said sternly.

'Agreed,' Wraith conceded, considering the humiliation

the knight had already suffered and the need to avoid further arguments against the larger numbers at Lockwood's command.

The knight smiled cruelly at her response before indicating in two directions across the ruins of Karnock.

'We will take the southern and western entrances, leaving the northern and eastern for you and your companions.'

'Very well,' Wraith agreed. 'Might I suggest that outside of the search of the mausoleum we adjoin forces to camp overnight. We have already learnt at the loss of several of your men of the dangers around us.'

'Two men and a squire,' Lockwood corrected.

'I am agreeable to uniting camps when needed,' Aederan said. 'There is safety in numbers.'

'Fine,' the knight said with frustration towards the elf. 'Now our business is complete, might we return to what brought us here and the contract I am paying you to complete?'

'As you order, my liege,' Aederan said with a bow.

Lockwood gave Wraith and Jaks one last derisory look before turning away and pacing towards his ruined camp. Several of the group followed the knight, as did the two young boys.

'Petero, you are to replace the fallen Damon as my scribe,' the knight ordered. 'I want a full account of our defeating the terrible hill giants, sparing little detail. I want the pages before nightfall, or your evening meal will be forfeit.'

'How did you end up with him?' Wraith asked Aederan once the knight was out of earshot. 'I thought the Lockwood who hired us was bad, but he is nothing on your knight.'

'A contract is a contract,' the elf conceded. 'The knight and his troop are, thankfully, temporary.'

'Thank the gods,' remarked a dwarven archer as he sauntered closer. Bronze circlets were in his hair and his splintmail armour was marked and damaged by years of combat. Beside him was a diminutive gnome with black hair parted by a white streak down the centre, and a bumbling female ogre standing a full head and shoulders above everyone. Wraith felt a sudden danger upon seeing the ogre, her kind known to be volatile and dangerous, but this one appeared far different, almost domesticated and friendly. Fenrix looked at the ogre and growled in warning, but all he did was earn himself a cheery laugh in return.

'Good dog,' the ogre said, reaching out to pet Fenrix before the weyre dived away.

'Badger, our gnome druid, Darsil Ulfgard, the best dwarven archer in the realms, and the big one, Axe, they're my group,' Aederan said. 'The rest are on Lockwood's payroll. We were hired to ensure success in finding the lance and protecting *his highness*.'

'I don't begrudge you your duties,' remarked Quinlan.

'We're already regretting it, aren't we?' Darsil the dwarf said as he hammered a fist onto Aederan's back. 'You promised me a fight, boss, and you didn't disappoint! Giants! Ha!'

'Raven, Fenrix, Quinlan, and Jakseyth,' the slayer introduced her group.

'Poor horse,' Axe, the female ogre, said sadly as she looked at the corpse half-eaten by the giants. She then looked up, sniffing the air and turning on Wraith.

'Smell troll blood on you,' she said with an uncertain expression, neither angry nor friendly. 'Troll distant kin of ogre.'

'I was forced to hunt one,' Wraith admitted. 'A Guild contract.'

'Was it good death?' Axe asked, her weapon tight in her grasp.

'He fought to the end.'

'Good,' Axe replied with a smile of rotting teeth. 'That's all any could want. That and ale.'

'I like her already,' Raven whispered.

The gnome of Aederan's group stepped forward and spoke in her own language, Wraith, Raven, Quinlan, Fenrix, and Jaks not understanding a single word. To them, it was a long tirade of gibberish.

'Badger here advises you to bring your horses into the courtyard,' Aederan explained. 'She says if she can smell the horses in the open, then so can those giants and any other that prey upon your steeds.'

'I will retrieve them,' Raven volunteered.

'And I will join you, Raven,' Aederan said, with a touch of his ruined ear. 'It has been some time since I have crossed paths with a fellow... well, let's just say someone who has shared experiences.'

Raven looked uncertain at first before finally relenting with a nod.

'In the meantime, perhaps a member of each party to keep watch,' Aederan suggested. 'We do not want those giants sneaking in again whilst we work.'

'Agreed,' Wraith said, looking over to Quinlan.

'Always happy to be volunteered,' the highborn said sarcastically as he reloaded his crossbows. 'I'll take the east.'

'I'll take the west,' Darsil, the dwarven archer, offered with wineskin clutched tight.

'Good,' Wraith replied. 'When we descend into the

tombs, we can have your knight post some of his men on watch.'

'Agreed, but first,' Aederan said with hushed words and a quick glance to ensure the knight and his cronies were not near, 'I'll warn you. We've already scouted all the entrances to the tombs beneath our feet. Our friend the knight has just left you with one entrance, the eastern. That's already been picked clean with no sign of the lance.'

'And the other?' Wraith asked.

'The northern entrance is completely blocked off by the rubble of the fallen keep.'

'That weaselly, conniving bastard,' Jaks seethed.

'He's highborn.' Quinlan chuckled. 'Of course he swindled us.'

'You haven't come across the Lavenell Lockwood tomb by chance?' Wraith asked.

'Not that I have seen, though any names and inscriptions are mostly lost to the sands of time,' the elven assassin explained.

'Thank you for the warning,' Raven said with a hint of a smile. 'The horses?'

'Lead on,' Aederan encouraged.

'Mine is to the north near that tower, if you wouldn't mind,' Jaks said, pointing the way.

'So, my family originated from the Allusyion Forest. How about you?' Aederan asked Raven as they walked away.

'Not there,' she replied.

'Did you ever find the villains who took you? I managed to escape my slavers, but I found them again.'

'Did you kill them?' Raven asked.

'Yes,' he said with a dark smile, 'but not before the lives of a great many of our kin had been ruined. I made them suffer for what they had done.'

'I dream of doing that very thing one day.'

Quinlan remained silent, watching as the elves departed before he paced towards the eastern side of the citadel and his post on watch.

'You didn't portal here from the citadel?' Wraith questioned.

'No, my dear,' the fiend replied.

'You could have just ridden or ran over here rather than use the portal,' Fenrix sneered.

'Yes, but where is the fun in that? You still have not warmed to me yet, have you? Tell me, is it the sorcerer or the fiend you distrust?'

'I care not for race,' the weyre replied. 'How could I? Look at me.'

'Then it is the arcane,' Wraith concluded.

'Sorcery made me... this,' he said with a raised, furred, clawed hand.

'And if it was within my power, I would undo it,' Jaks swore, 'but I am afraid this is nothing I have come across in my studies.'

'No one can help me,' Fenrix murmured.

'But you can help us,' Wraith said. 'The eastern tombs have already been plundered, so that leaves us with the northern. It was that very entrance that the viscount, our employer, advised. We can put your strength to good use, Fenrix. Get us through the rubble of this accursed fortress.'

'I can help with that too,' Jaks said with a smile and flicker of arcane in the eyes.

'Let's get to work,' Wraith ordered before pausing for a moment. She thought she heard a voice on the wind, distant and lost.

'Welcome.'

CHAPTER ELEVEN
THE RUINED FORTRESS OF KARNOCK

THE LOCKWOOD MAUSOLEUM - NORTHERN TOMBS

Wraith and Raven had scouted the area, picking their way through the rubble of fallen stone walls and broken masonry until they could estimate the location of the northern entrance to the mausoleum below. With a location decided, the combined might of Jaks and Fenrix was put to task, tearing through the fallen ruin of Karnock's Keep. The weyre heaved broken walls of stone, tossing what he could aside with brute strength until he was panting for breath. The sorcerer made the very ground beneath them rise to shift aside obstructions in their path, and with other abilities, lifted stone and rock without touch. Wraith, Raven, and Quinlan, once his watch was complete with no sighting of the giants, helped where they could, but their contributions were minimal in comparison. After some time and with the sun beginning to set behind them, a small gap in the stone and rock could be seen that led to descending stairs into the ground; an entrance to the Lockwood vault.

'I think we can all squeeze through,' Quinlan said with a questioning look at Wraith.

'I will fit just fine,' the weyre growled.

'I thought your arcane was just ice?' Wraith questioned as Jaks took a seat amongst the ruin, breathing heavily, her skin covered in sweat from her efforts. Raven offered the bottle of wine she had been drinking from, the elf's own preparations for the descent beneath them, but the fiend took out her own flask of water, drinking deep.

'Ice comes naturally to me,' the sorcerer replied. 'It is of my homeland of Ithandyr, a realm of snow and ice. Other spells and arcana take more focus and learning. Though I now stand an acolyte of the order, I still learn and grow.'

'You lifted the stone with your mind?' Quinlan asked.

'Impressed?'

'Something like that.' The highborn looked to the dark and haunting stairwell. 'We really going down there?'

'Sure are,' Raven said with a forced smile, followed by another swig from her bottle.

As Jakseyth and Fenrix recovered from their efforts, Wraith, Raven, and Quinlan made their preparations. Raven saw to her two curved knives, but also to the elven bow recovered from Stonemere. Over a shoulder, she carried a quiver of black feathered arrows. Quinlan oiled and reloaded both of his light-crossbows and then saw to the blade of his rapier. Wraith checked over her weapons and tools; the shortsword marked with the faint arrow-head outline, the silver dagger given by the Guild, the throwing knives, potions and vials purchased, the thieving tools and lockpicks from her Guild training. Lastly were the torches, a pair pulled from Raven's pack. She lit one with a flint, letting the flames grow before throwing the torch through the small gap in the stone and rock, lighting the way ahead and down into the darkness.

'Ladies first,' Quinlan offered once Jaks and Wraith rose to their feet, ready.

'Coward,' Raven teased, but it was Wraith who stepped forward first.

Squeezing between the broken rubble, grazing against the stonework that once formed a mighty, towering keep, the slayer dropped down to the descending staircase. Her boots landed on debris, and she slipped, falling several steps until she could catch herself before she could fall to the bottom. Wraith descended farther, picking up the aflame torch and clambering past the rubble in her path. Deeper and deeper the stairs took her until, at the very bottom, she found a rusted and aged set of iron gates, torn free by time and the ruin above.

With torch raised, she looked upon the catacombs ahead of her, likely the first for over a hundred years to set foot in the Lockwood mausoleum. The crypt split into two, a path to the left and right. Within each was row upon row upon row of granite columns stretched out into the darkness, alcoves formed at the walls, each housing a tomb to the fallen Lockwood lineage. Some had statues with likenesses of the lords and ladies of the entombed, and near every tomb in sight was engraved with the Lockwood coat of arms of raised sword. This place was old, silent, and forgotten; a tomb in every sense of the word.

One by one, Raven, Jaks, Quinlan, and then Fenrix joined her at the bottom of the staircase, the weyre looking worse for wear, the fur and skin torn bloody at his shoulder and back.

'What happened?' Wraith asked with concern.

'It was a tighter squeeze than I thought,' Fenrix grunted.

Jaks tapped the butt of her spear to the stone floor, a

flare of purple light emanating and illuminating from its three points.

'There are two things I dislike in this world,' the she-elf said as she lit her torch on Wraith's. 'The underground and fire.'

Without warning, Fenrix smashed his axe into a nearby wall, crushing a spider the size of his fist. 'And I dislike spiders,' he growled as he wiped the axe clean.

'You have any of that wine left?' Quinlan asked as he peered into the silent, haunting darkness around them.

'Not for you,' the elf replied, handing the highborn the aflame torch.

'Don't you need it?'

'Elvish eyes can see far better in the darkness than humans.'

'As can wolf,' Fenrix added, pushing Quinlan from behind to urge him on.

'Look.' Jaks pointed to the stonework around the arch entrance. There were engravings around them, runes and glyphs, words of a dozen languages, much faded and lost to the passage of time. At the centre where the arch passed over their heads was the Lockwood symbol of a raised sword.

'You think that's the lance?' Raven asked, her words uncertain and shaky, wary of the enclosed surroundings underground.

'Elven, dwarven, fiend, common, gnomish,' Quinlan recounted as he looked to the markings. 'There are even passages from the ancients.'

'Can you read it?' Wraith asked.

'From my studies as a child. Languages was the one lesson my tutors had no problem retaining my attention in.'

'The hardships of wealth,' Raven teased. 'How did you become a bandit again?'

'A story for another time.' Quinlan gave a wry grin as he continued looking at the runes.

'Can you read it?' Wraith repeated.

'Much of it is gone,' Quinlan said, 'but I can patch some of it together… like a puzzle, I guess.'

'What does it say?' Jaks asked.

'Welcome to the lair of Daegon,' Quinlan read. 'Respect the honoured dead of Lockwood.'

None spoke then at the mention of Daegon, God of death and the afterlife. This was his domain, as was any crypt or mausoleum beneath the earth.

Wraith placed a hand to the arrowhead pendant at her chest for luck as she and the others passed the fallen and entered the Lockwood Mausoleum. All of them, having taken a single step, came to a resounding halt.

As they crossed the threshold, Wraith felt a dreading chill creep over her skin. Looking at the others, she saw they had all been touched by the sudden wave of fear and horror. Wraith and Raven shuddered, Quinlan groaned with disgust, Fenrix growled feral, and the shimmering light from Jaks's spear and eyes flickered brightly.

'*Welcome,*' called a voice heard by not the ears, but the minds of each of them.

'Anyone else hear that?' Wraith asked.

'Yes,' Raven, Fenrix, Quinlan, and Jaks all replied, haunted and shaken.

'What was that?' Raven asked. 'Daegon?'

'We are in his realm now,' Jaks said. 'But I do not think he would trifle with the likes of us mortals.'

'Let's hope not.' Wraith summoned her courage and led on, pointing her torch to the path on the right. 'I will take this side, half of you, that side. Keep your eyes alert for the sword... the lance... whatever it is, and whatever surprises await us down here. We don't know what the Lockwoods have done to protect their ancestors. Don't touch anything. That goes double for you, Quinlan.'

'Fine by me,' he muttered.

'Lord Lavenell Lockwood is the tomb we seek,' Wraith instructed. 'The lance is interred in his tomb.'

The group split, Wraith and Jaks taking one side of the catacombs, and Raven, Quinlan, and Fenrix taking the other. Both parties walked slowly, passing between the columns and inspecting the tombs. On one side, Fenrix and Quinlan spoke, trying to ease their fears, but also trying to ease those of Raven, the elf looking uncomfortable. Wraith and Jaks did much the same as they began their search.

'As you likely guessed, I received your letter, my dear liberator,' Jaks said to the slayer.

'You wouldn't be here if not,' Wraith replied.

'Your warning was appreciated also, of the dead Sacred sorcerers.'

'Did you find them?'

'Not yet,' Jaks confessed. 'The Skypeaks are vast, and it will take time with the rest blizzards.'

'They were searching for Blain Ironhill, weren't they? Still no sign of the dwarf?'

The dwarf she spoke of was one of the few survivors of the terrors of Stonemere. Originally recruited by Wraith, Blain Ironhill travelled with the party to the cursed village. Once they had encountered the horrors that had taken the region, the dwarf abandoned Wraith and her group, but not before pocketing an amulet of dark occult power. The last Wraith had heard, the Sacred was searching for Blain, believing the amulet to be directly adjoined to the evil Wraith and her allies had purged.

'None, except the trail of bodies left in his wake,' the fiend said with sorrow. 'All sent to hunt him down have not returned alive.'

'I've heard that name again,' Wraith said. 'Axuroth, from a troll in the mountains. Have you uncovered anything about it yet?'

Jaks paused for a moment, concern in her eyes. 'I promise you, we will talk once away from this haunted place.'

They continued to walk slowly through the crypt, their footsteps echoing in all directions. The flames of her torch and the light from atop Jaks's spear flickered and cast light ahead of them, but did not penetrate the darkness completely. The shadows shifted and moved, playing tricks on the mind.

Around them, the tombs lay undisturbed and at peace, stone caskets and statues preserved by the fallen keep above and the blocked entrance. Each tomb was different, the stone caskets chiselled and engraved with names, patterns, and runes unique to each of the interned. Gentle and fair statues of the womenfolk and honourable and heroic of the men. Items were laid out around and atop the tombs, personal effects and possessions or tokens given by loved ones. Rings, circlets, weapons, feathers, frozen flowers and leaves, and jewels reminded that this place was both to honour the dead and for those to pay their respects to the lost. Wraith felt a sudden guilt, intruding in this place of honour.

'Do not be concerned,' Jaks said, guessing the doubts of the slayer. 'We are here to fulfil a contract, nothing more. Unlike others, we are no grave-robbers.'

'Agreed,' Wraith said gratefully. 'Thank you for coming to our aid. I know as a newly appointed acolyte you must be busy.'

'Never too busy for you. If not for you and your friends, I would still be in capacity... or far worse. I am forever indebted to you, as are many of our group.'

'Thank you,' Wraith said again before looking at her hands and feeling a dull ache at the joints. 'Tell me, what is life like in the citadel?'

'I was taken in as a child,' the fiend explained, surprised by the question. 'I came from a happy home and family. My talent was noticed early, and I was called up.'

'Did you have a choice?'

'It was expected. My father was a sorcerer, and in my race, the arcane lineage is strong. I was prepared.'

'Did you have a choice?' Wraith repeated, the fiend's silence answer enough.

'My tutors in the Sacred were firm but fair,' Jaks eventually said. 'Study was constant and arduous, with failure punished and no quarter given for falling behind.'

Much like the Guild, Wraith thought.

'Then I was apprenticed with Imperator Deytrum Vaas, and my path took me to the little village of Stonemere,' Jaks continued. 'Now, I am here.'

'Would you change any of it?'

'Perhaps, but I am happy for where my path has taken me.'

'I am glad to have you with us,' Wraith said, despite the hidden risks the sorcerer's presence brought. Wraith's secret, the arcane power within; any discovery would lead to the ruin of not just her but all those she cared for.

'What of you?' Jaks asked. 'Are you content?'

Wraith thought of her past, her training with the Guild, their tests and assessments and unending trials. She thought of Guildmaster Brevik, her only family, a secret in its own right, and one of the few who gave her any form of affection. She allowed her memories to drift further, but they brought her to that fateful night amidst the flames and snow when her family and home were ripped from her amidst the blood of betrayal.

As if fated, her eyes fell upon the arrowhead symbol of the Athscar family engraved upon a tomb. Wraith blinked furiously, believing it to be an illusion or trick of the mind, but reaching out, she felt the stone carving. She stepped back in shock, quickly looking towards a row of tombs and urns that ended the crypt and joined where Raven, Quinlan, and Fenrix approached. Wraith looked closer to the urns and saw there were many different emblems and coats-of-arms, many family names buried within the crypt.

'My dear, what alarms you?' Jakseyth asked.

'These… these are different,' Wraith said. 'These are not of the Lockwood family.'

'The honoured dead,' Quinlan explained as the second group approached. 'Those who fought alongside the Lockwoods and died here during the Dark Days.'

'Heroes,' Raven said.

Wraith looked to each of the tombs and urns, seeing dozens of them stretching out as far as their light sources could illuminate. There were no names, but she recognised some of the emblems and family symbols, though many were a mystery, lost to time and tragedy. There were roaring beasts, proud animals, charging knights, and crossed blades. Upon the tombs themselves were shields, pieces of armour, spears, swords, and actual lances. One urn was surrounded by arrows, dedicated to an archer. A worn set of dice rested; a gambler, perhaps. One stone casket was covered in fangs and horns, tokens of the beasts the honoured dead had slain in their life. Another was surrounded by the weaponry of orcs, ogres, reptilians, and more; the arms of vanquished foes. Upon one casket was a four-leaf clover symbol of luck and a small portrait of a wife and daughter.

Seeing the portrait, Wraith was reminded of her own family and her eyes returned to the Athscar arrowhead. This was one of her ancestors. A pain hit her within; sorrow, loss, regret, and lastly, shame.

'We will take nothing from here,' Wraith declared. 'We will leave this place as we found it, undisturbed.'

'But Lady Lockwood said she would pay for Lockwood artefacts,' Quinlan said.

'Not these ones,' Wraith said firmly.

'He's not here,' Raven conceded, the discomfort and unease she felt below ground clear to all.

'Lord Lavenell Lockwood must be elsewhere,' Jaks confirmed.

'Damn it. I felt certain that of all places, this would be the one,' Quinlan said.

'Agreed,' Wraith said.

'We are long into the night now,' Fenrix warned.

'Let us return to the camp above.' Wraith earned an approving and enthusiastic nod of approval from Raven. 'Rest and sleep and begin anew tomorrow.'

Wraith, unseen by the others, placed a hand upon the stone engraving of the arrowhead again for just a moment. Her eyes closed, thoughts returning to her lost mother and father, brothers and sisters. Thoughts returned to all that was taken from her, a single tear falling to her cheek. She felt Raven's hand take hers, squeezing for a moment in comfort. Only the elf understood the pain Wraith felt, for she was there that night when so much was lost. Wraith gripped Raven's hand before releasing, her fingertips finding their way to the arrowhead pendant at her chest.

'I remember,' she whispered to the Athscar family.

Gladdened by the moment, Wraith's eyes opened, and

she lifted her hand from the tomb. No sooner had her fingers left the stone, then there was a loud, sudden knocking.

'What did you touch?' Raven accused Quinlan.

'Nothing… I don't think,' the highborn said defensively.

'We should not have come here,' Fenrix snarled as he looked for the origin of the sounds.

'We should leave this place,' Jaks said with eyes to the crypt's floor, hearing movement.

'Back away!' Wraith yelled as the sounds grew closer and closer. 'Back away from the tombs!'

Suddenly, from the floor around every single tomb in the Lockwood vault, rose rows of deadly spears, narrowly missing the group as they hurried back. The knocking began above them until spears fell from the crypt ceiling. Wraith and Raven dove away, finding shelter beneath an arch. Jaks lifted her own spear, a dome of purple light shimmering above and deflecting several of the falling missiles. Fenrix was not so fortunate, nor was Quinlan. The weyre was struck twice, a spear tearing across his thigh and another ripping through his arm. The highborn was more blessed, suffering only a tear through his waist-coat across the chest.

'I just repaired this,' Quinlan said with disgust.

'You're lucky it wasn't your head,' Wraith replied.

'I wasn't so lucky,' Fenrix whimpered, wincing as he staggered.

There was no time to see to his wounds, as again, knocking sounded throughout the mausoleum. A howling rush of air extinguished both the torches, the flames gone and leaving Jak's staff as the only source of dim light. Wraith's eyes adjusted, her training with the Guild heightening her senses in the darkness. The voice then returned in their minds, but no words this time, only sinister, sickening laughter.

'Show yourself!' Fenrix roared, but there was no reply or sound but for the growing knock above and below them. A hiss sounded from ahead of them, and then from behind and across the floor. Rising quickly was a thick green gas.

'Don't breathe it in,' Jaks warned.

'Back to the staircase,' Wraith ordered. 'Run!'

They fled, covering their mouths and running with all haste, struggling not to breathe or inhale the rising gas. When they were halfway, a clicking sounded from behind them, above the urns of heroes. Wraith turned, and though she could not see in the darkness, she could not mistake the sound of flint striking. A flicker of a spark, an ember that ignited the gas.

'RUN!' she screamed as the flames spread and surged towards them.

The staircase was ahead, and though they were near, they would not reach it before the flames engulfed them. Raven was quickest and nearest to the stairs. Fenrix grabbed hold of Wraith and Quinlan and leapt forward, the injuries from the spears forgotten as the need to flee took hold. Jaks was last, and just before the flames could reach her, she turned to face them, eyes flickering with arcane as a wall of frost rose like a shield. The inferno slammed into the ice, the force of the explosion throwing the party forward.

They landed at the bottom of the stone staircase, Quinlan upside down a few steps up with Raven just below him, Wraith buried beneath Fenrix, and Jaks at the bottom of the stairs. The inferno had died down as the gas burnt away, leaving ash in the air and the tombs utterly undisturbed, protecting the dead.

'I have certainly missed you all,' Jaks laughed as she patted out the flames on her robes without concern.

Quinlan coughed and looked at them in surprise, still upside down. Fenrix moved aside, helping Wraith up before patting out the embers of flames amongst his fur. Raven pushed them aside and trampled over Quinlan, pale and gasping for breath, fleeing up the staircase. Worried, Wraith followed her, ascending the staircase quickly and then squeezing through the rubble of the keep, welcomed by the darkness of night and the stars above.

Sat amongst the broken stone was the she-elf, hyperventilating and shaking.

'You're fine. You're fine.' Wraith tried to calm her, arms wrapping around Raven to comfort her. The elf said nothing, skin still trembling for her ordeal underground and the horror of flames. Her eyes clamped shut and elvish words escaped her lips, lost in terror.

'Step aside,' Quinlan said firmly to Wraith as he joined them, ash covering every inch of him. Gently, he eased Wraith's grip from the elf before seating himself opposite Raven and taking her hands in his own.

'Raven,' he said calmly. 'You are outside, in the open, free and safe. We are with you, your... friends. Keep your eyes closed. Empty your mind. Focus on your breathing. Breathe with me. In... and... out. You are free. You are safe.'

Raven's breathing calmed and her head lowered.

'Here, drink this,' Quinlan said, handing her a small flask. Raven drank, then recoiled at its strength.

'Good huh,' the noble grinned. 'You know, I won this in a card game against a deposed king and a...'

'Thank you,' Raven said, throwing the flask back to him.

'Take your time,' Wraith said with a reassuring hand on the elf's shoulder.

'Let's never go back down into that one,' the elf said.

'Agreed,' the slayer said.

'Agreed,' Quinlan added.

'Definitely.' Jaks joined them, tired and still trying to extinguish the embers burning at her robes.

Fenrix did not say a word as he approached them, smoke still rising from his scorched fur as he slumped to the ground and looked at the stars and the moon above. The weyre winced with every breath and movement, wounded by spears, flames, and merely squeezing through the stone rubble twice, along with the wounds taken in facing the giants.

'You look as bad as I feel, wolfie,' Raven called to him.

'Worse,' he growled.

'Perhaps our friends in the camp have a healer for you,' Quinlan said.

'Or I have a potion I could spare you,' Wraith offered.

'Later,' the weyre replied. 'I don't want to move right now.'

Jaks approached Wraith and spoke quietly, unheard by the others.

'That was just the first of the vaults of this mausoleum,' the fiend warned. 'I can see now why so many have not returned from this place.'

'Joining the dead beneath us,' Wraith agreed, still haunted by the sinister laughter they all heard in the darkness.

CHAPTER TWELVE

THE RUINED FORTRESS OF KARNOCK

For the night, a member of Wraith's, Aederan's, and Sir Antonius Lockwood's group provided the guard and kept watch for the giants and any other threats. The groups mostly kept to themselves, although all could hear the blustering of Sir Antonius as he barked orders at his squires and hired cronies. Food was prepared and eaten, the past day's exploits discussed and plans made for what they would do come morning. Wraith and her group had already decided the northern crypts housed nothing of worth and would remain sealed away and forgotten, once Fenrix and Jaks had the strength to block the entrance once again. Instead, they would focus on the eastern tombs, despite the warning that they had already been plundered. Their hope was that they could find something, anything, that had been missed.

All but Jaks had fed on the rabbits and birds hunted by Raven in the nearby woods, the fiend preferring the vegetables and herbs she brought in her pack to the offered meat. The sorcerer sat with eyes closed in a peaceful trance, and

Quinlan worked on his crossbows, applying oil to the mechanisms. Raven had eagerly taken her turn on watch, keen to avoid her companions after the harrowing events earlier. Fenrix snored gently by the fire. The weyre's injuries had been seen to by the gnome known as Badger, despite his snarled protests. The druid had applied ointments and salves to his wounds, muttering her language with all nearby oblivious to her meaning. Fenrix was given a concoction and quickly fell to slumber curled up by the warmth of the fire, Badger fast asleep with her head leant against the wolf's back.

Wraith sat by her party's campfire, readying her equipment for the coming day; a habit when trying to control nerves. What they had seen in the northern crypt and their escape weighed heavy on their minds, as did the voice they had heard. The most shocking of all the discoveries to her though, was the Athscar tomb, the grave of one of her ancestors. She could discuss it with no one, not even Raven, who knew of her haunted past but did not want to talk to anyone at this time. The Slayer lifted her shortsword to the light, gazing upon the barely visible arrowhead symbol etched into the blade. Memories long forgotten of family and home kept coming to her. She could see their faces, hear their voices, and recalled their names for the first time since that terrible night in the snow. Instinctively, her hand found its way to her arrowhead pendant.

'I heard tales that this place was haunted,' Quinlan said as he pulled free a part of the crossbow mechanism and scrubbed it clean. 'Ghosts of the dead from the Dark Days battles, or the slaughter of the Lockwoods. You think that was the voice we heard down there?'

'Perhaps,' Wraith said, lost in her own thoughts.

'If you look to the battlements, there are shadows

moving,' Jaks said, with eyes still closed. 'Spirits linger, tied to this realm and unable to escape.'

'What, really?' The highborn nervously looked around them.

'And watching us this very moment,' the sorcerer said with a smile on her lips.

'Are they hostile?' he asked as he hastily attempted to rebuild his crossbows.

'She's teasing you,' Wraith said. 'The shadows are merely that. Shadows.'

'Spoilsport,' remarked Jaks.

'Great,' Quinlan snapped as he threw down his crossbows. 'Just great. Now I have to start over with these again. You know, where I'm from, no one would show respect to a member of the Clysley name.'

'Lucky for us, we aren't there then,' Wraith joked.

'I think you're just prickly because our elven friend is on watch with the other elf around here,' Jaks said. 'A charming fellow, he is.'

'I have no idea what you're talking about,' Quinlan mumbled as he recovered one of the crossbows and began working at the mechanism again.

'Are you certain?' Wraith asked. 'That was impressive how you calmed her.'

'It was merely something I learned as a child,' he replied, looking into the flames of the fire. 'My little sister, she had an affliction that claimed her courage and sanity, not too dissimilar to our elf.'

'If I didn't know better, I would have thought it some lower magic or healing,' Jaks said, the sorcerer impressed too.

'No. It was merely something the family physician showed me long ago to calm.'

'Family physician, highborn name, once fancy clothes,

and from what appears up close to be expensive crossbows,' Jaks remarked. 'Can I assume it is not by choice that you turned commoner rather than remain a Clibbsly?'

'Clysley,' Quinlan corrected, though he left the fiend's question unanswered.

Fenrix snored loudly by the fire, the gnome potion leaving him deep in slumber. Badger was startled for a moment before nuzzling into the weyre's fur as she softly hummed a tune.

'I have wondered... why do you carry two crossbows into combat?' Wraith asked Quinlan. 'After the initial bolts are loosed, you can only wield one of the weapons in order to reload.'

'Two bolts are better than one,' he remarked. 'Even if it is just the once.'

'They're a fine set you have,' Wraith said, guilty for the earlier taunts.

'For the painful memories they create, I should cast them into the fire, but I can't bring myself to do it. A haunting of my own, perhaps.'

'You don't need to tell us,' Wraith assured.

'It might help.' He sighed heavily, eyes remaining on the crossbow in his hands as he worked and talked. 'My younger brother, Nathaniel, it was his challenge that drove me from home. That and the damnation of my father. A duel to the death was to determine who would become heir to the family leadership. I was to choose the weapons, and my choice was crossbows. This very set. We were to fight at dawn, but cowardice took me. I disappeared in the night, stealing the crossbows as I fled. For that, I was shamed and banished, warned never to return and never to draw upon the family name.'

'I'm sorry,' Wraith said, suddenly realising the painful origin of so much of the man's character.

'And what followed was a treacherous path of booze, women, gambling, and worse, I imagine,' Jaks said, with eyes still closed.

'Couldn't have put it better myself,' Quinlan agreed with a forced smile.

'Well met, fellow explorers,' Aederan greeted as he and the dwarven archer Darsil approached and took the offered seats by the fire. 'My turn on watch passed uneventfully, but I was in fine company with your friend, Raven.'

'How is she?' Quinlan asked.

'Quiet,' Aederan replied. 'Is that common?'

'Sometimes,' Wraith said, though she was concerned.

'We left her with Axe, though I doubt our bumbling ogre will bring much of a smile to her,' the elf said. 'Who'd have thought one of her kind could be afraid of the dark!'

'She thinks this place is cursed,' Darsil murmured.

'Axe thinks everywhere we go is cursed,' Aederan countered. 'She is more scared of this place than those poor boy squires our knight yells at day and night. She's gruff but trustworthy. Names herself after whatever weapon she carries. Today she is Axe.'

'How did you come to be in the company of that... thing?' Quinlan asked.

'Known her since she was young,' Darsil explained between swigs from a flask. 'Family slain and village destroyed. We took her in when others wanted to put her to the sword.'

'Unfortunate souls have a way of finding me.' Aederan pretended to grimace.

'I know the feeling.' Wraith smiled, with looks at Quinlan, Jaks, and the sleeping Fenrix. 'Our day was wasted, and we remain empty-handed, but for some fresh scars. Did you have any better fortune?'

'Sadly not,' the elven assassin admitted as he took a seat near to them. 'We took to the western entrance first, but all we found were preparation chambers. There was nothing of real interest. A priest's quarters, some half constructed stone caskets, empty urns, and of course, tools for preparing bodies for internment.'

'Nothing of worth, and no sign of the lance,' Darsil said as the dwarf twirled an arrow between his fingers.

'Fascinating,' Quinlan remarked dismissively as he set to work on his crossbows again.

'The southern entrance promised more,' Aederan said.

'Oh yeah,' Darsil said as he edged the tip of his arrow into the fire, letting the feather flights catch light.

'The initial crypts had already been thoroughly looted,' Aederan explained. 'And from the bodies we found, we knew this mausoleum was not undefended.'

'Bodies?' Wraith asked.

'Looters,' Aederan replied. 'Graverobbers…'

'Us,' Darsil added with a chuckle.

'Guild members,' the elf agreed.

'You're certain?' Wraith asked.

'We saw their brandings,' Aederan said with a tap to his arm. 'We counted at least eight bodies just in the first chambers we came across. Trap, beast, or rival the causes by our guess.'

'More traps,' Wraith said, pointing to Fenrix. 'We encountered a few live ones of our own.'

'As did we. Lockwood lost a couple of his hired guard to them, but my lot were lucky and not a scratch amongst us.'

'There can only be traps to protect something,' Darsil said with a grin as he weaved patterns in the air with his aflame arrow.

'The honoured Lockwood dead?' Jaks commented, with eyes still closed.

'Something of worth and value is my bet,' the dwarf replied. 'Coin aplenty for all.'

'We can only hope,' Aederan agreed. 'We found a few baubles and gems, but most of it was personal items or weapons aged beyond use. There were a couple of items that may be of worth.'

From his pocket, the elf pulled a cloth wrapped tight. Carefully, he unfastened the cloth, making sure not to touch the contents, a simple golden band, a circlet. Darsil then pulled out a simple silver dagger, the design instantly recognisable to Wraith.

'A guild blade,' she said, taking the dagger and lifting it up to view.

'Just like those gifted to apprentices to complete their trials,' Aederan agreed as he drew his own for comparison. It was identical, all except for the single letter engraved on the pommel, an L upon the recovered blade.

'Luthor,' Wraith said, the name escaping her lips with excitement and then horrible certainty. He was here. 'Did you find a body?'

'None with that blade,' Darsil commented as he hastily snatched the dagger from Wraith and fastened it away, not wanting to lose one of their few finds.

Wraith's mind raced both with possibility and doom. *Luthor was here, but what happened to him. Has he lost his life in the darkness of the crypts, body remaining with the rest of the entombed? Could he have survived and fled this terrible place?*

'Who is Luthor?' Aederan asked.

'A question I too have asked before,' Quinlan added.

Wraith was silent for a moment, looking into the flames of the campfire before speaking. 'Luthor and I were both apprentices of the Guild. We were… close.'

'Lovers?' Darsil suggested.

'No, just friends,' Wraith said. 'When I came to the guild, I was a young girl with nothing. No family and not a penny to my name. Luthor was the only one who showed me any kindness.'

'Did he know your name?' Quinlan asked. 'Your real name, I mean? He must have been something special if he knew that.'

'We endured everything our training could throw at us,' Wraith continued, ignoring the highborn's questioning. 'Not long ago, we set out for our trials to earn our place in the Guild. Luthor never returned, but I believe that was his dagger.'

'Perhaps your boy is here, perhaps not,' Darsil said as he wiped the silver blade clean and tucked it away in his belongings. 'Perhaps he was one of the many fools who have lost their lives here in pursuit of treasure.'

'Just like us?' Wraith asked as she struggled to keep her calm against the dwarf's words.

'How long you been with the Guild?' Aederan asked Wraith with a tap of his brand. 'Formally, I mean?'

'Not long. This is only my third contract.'

'Starting at the top.' The elf admired. 'Bravery or foolishness, I wonder. No offence.'

'Neither. It was a challenge without choice. How long have you been with the Guild in Aelthorn?'

'Twelve years this summer,' Aederan said, with a touch of his burnt ears. 'It was how I earned my freedom. We have completed countless contracts ranging from simple requests of lords to audiences with our own honourable King Rothgard.'

'And is it bravery or foolishness that brings you here?'

'Empty pockets,' Darsil answered for him.

'My dwarven friend is sadly right,' the assassin said.

'Our purse grows lighter by the day, but Lockwood's coin will last our group near a year once we have it.'

'How much is he paying?' Quinlan asked with wonder.

'Plenty.' Darsil grinned, revealing a few golden teeth among his smile. 'Plus whatever loot we find, besides the lance.'

'Speaking of loot, what of the circlet?' Quinlan asked as he lifted a hand towards it.

'Don't,' Aederan warned. 'Do not touch it. The last man who did lost a hand.'

'A bit much to fight over a simple gold band.'

'You misunderstand me,' the elf said. 'The man who found this, one of Lockwood's, placed the band upon his wrist. Within moments, the hand beneath withered and blackened with corruption. We took the arm in an attempt to stop the rot, but we fear it had already taken a deeper hold. He collapsed shortly after and has not woken since.'

'May I?' Jaks asked, eyes opening with fascination.

'Don't touch it,' Aederan warned as he carefully lifted the cloth and its contents and placed it into the sorcerer's waiting hands.

'Do you know of such things?' Wraith asked.

'No, not yet,' the fiend replied as her eyes shimmered and shifted, flashing with violet light as she studied the artefact. It was the same ability the fence had displayed at the Guild. 'With the arcane, I can see into the core of an object. Its origin and purpose.'

'Impressive,' Quinlan remarked with wonder.

'There are others who can do far more than I,' Jaks said. 'Transmutation, illusion, enchantment, conjuration… the list goes on. I have learnt but a sample of what there is.'

'And what does your sample tell you about our piece of gold here?' Darsil asked.

'As you likely guessed, this circlet carries a curse,' the fiend explained as her eyes ceased to shimmer and calmed. 'Crafted for the sole purpose of corrupting those with greed in their eyes and hearts. Its placement here was to protect the grave of a loved one and punish those who would disturb their rest.'

'You can keep that,' Aederan said, as Jaks offered back the artefact.

'I could have been lying, you know,' she teased.

'The effect it had was no lie. If you ask me, Axe might have been right. This place is cursed... and you know what I am talking about, Aederan.'

The elf looked away dismissively.

'Did you hear anything down there?' Wraith asked. 'Voices?'

The haunted look Darsil gave her was answer enough.

'We heard laughter,' Aederan said. 'Whenever one of our group fell or was maimed, it came, mocking us.'

At that exact moment, a sudden gust of wind rose and blew harsh, almost extinguishing the campfire and sweeping around them before falling still and silent.

'Well, I've had enough of this place,' Quinlan said, certainly spooked by their surroundings and what lay beneath their feet in the crypts below.

'You're not the only one,' Darsil said. 'No booze and no ladyfolk but for those with your party.'

'You'll have all the drink and company you want with the reward for Lockwood's prize,' Aederan encouraged.

'That's saying you reach it first,' challenged Quinlan, drawing a long grin from the elf and loud, mocking laughter from the dwarf.

'Not being funny, but look at your pitiful band.' Darsil cheered. 'Apart from the sorcerer, what have you got?'

'We have enough, dwarf,' Jaks sneered.

'And what did you say, this was your second contract?' Darsil asked.

'Third,' Wraith said, though quickly realised she had not exactly helped their case.

'Third.' The dwarf laughed some more. 'That is a very big step up to... well, all this. You will be lucky to survive, let alone find the prize.'

'So we keep being told,' Wraith replied. 'No one believes in us and no one would bet on us. That is why we will succeed.'

'Well said,' Jaks remarked.

'I would bet on us,' Quinlan said. 'Darsil, care for coin to determine what your words have started?'

'Never turned down a bet before.' The dwarven archer grinned.

'Fifty gold says we find the lance first,' Quinlan said.

'Make it one hundred,' the dwarf replied. 'Or might two hundred better fit the size of this task... if you have it.'

'Darsil...' Aederan warned, but his companion ignored him.

Quinlan looked uncertain at first, the sum greater than the highborn expected.

'If you're so certain of your... *abilities*, then you should have no issue,' Darsil said with a cruel smirk. 'Or perhaps I was right about you.'

'Two hundred,' Wraith suddenly agreed, angered by the dwarf's assumptions. Darsil took her hand quickly in agreement, his grin unflinching.

'Just think of all the company I could afford with our reward and my winnings,' the dwarf taunted.

'That's if any of us find the lance,' Wraith said.

'And how long do we keep looking if each day we have nothing to show for our efforts?' Darsil asked. 'For all we know, the Lockwood Lance is long gone from here, or was only a fable all along.'

'You should know we won't be leaving,' Aederan said 'We don't leave a contract unfinished.'

Quinlan looked to Wraith, who merely shook her head. They weren't going anywhere either.

'All this for one lance,' the highborn remarked. 'What a stupid name anyway, lance. It's a sword, plain and simple...'

'Do not speak of what you know nothing about, you penniless fool,' a commanding voice ordered as Sir Antonius Lockwood approached. Behind him was an escort of the red-skinned, long-horned fiend and a pair of human thugs.

'Do not speak to my friend like that,' Jaks warned, eyes closed in a trance again.

'It is you who should not speak with such disregard to Sir Antonius,' the red-skinned fiend snarled with fangs on show and a hand upon the hilt of a blade at his side. 'Or are manners beyond you?'

'That's rich coming from a savage like you.' Jaks's eyes flashed open and narrowed on her brethren.

'Enough!' Sir Antonius ordered to the fiend at his side. 'Enough, Skiminos. This is not the reason I approached. Aederan, I would make plans with you for the coming day. We have only explored a small portion of the southern crypts with much more to be searched. They will release their secrets and we will find the lance.'

'Sir, today you lost two of your men and one of your squires to the giants,' Aederan began. 'We then lost three more in the tombs below. Are you certain this is what you want?'

'Those who died lost their lives due to idiocy and greed. We are better without them.'

One of the squires sniffed then, tears in his eyes. The boy's face was red from more than tears, a bruise forming around one eye.

'Enough of your snivelling, Mason,' Sir Antonius snapped. 'Only women sob. Your brother Damon is gone. Steel yourself and have courage or you will meet the same fate.'

'Tomorrow, we press ahead, despite the dangers?' Aederan asked.

'Petero,' the knight called to his second squire and appointed scribe, 'note this for the account. We will honour our lost this night, but tomorrow we will succeed where we failed this day.'

Wraith saw Aederan and Darsil share a look of warning.

'Now, my elven friend, return to our camp, where we shall make plans,' Lockwood ordered. 'Let us leave this rabble to their much needed slumber.'

'My apologies,' Aederan said as he slowly rose up and followed his master as he marched away. Skiminos, the fiend, shot one last filthy look at Jaks before he too followed the knight and his entourage.

'Charming company we have here,' remarked Wraith once their guests were gone.

'Scharbaxians,' Jaks spat. 'Deceitful, red-skinned demons. I am not surprised Sir Antonius has one of them in his service.'

'Not all are like that,' Wraith argued, thinking of Cavluva, her friend at the guild.

'True, but this one seems to only confirm the opinion that all fiends are cheating, devilish scoundrels.'

'I bet he is saying the same of you right now,' Quinlan commented.

'I do not doubt it.' She unexpectedly chuckled. 'The

clans of my kind have always been divided by more than just the colour of our skin. Prejudice, fear, and war is our past.'

'But it does not need to be your future,' Wraith suggested.

'Well said,' Jaks said.

'Quinlan,' Wraith said. 'It's time you relieved Raven on watch.'

'Just so,' he agreed, securing his crossbows to his belt and draining his canteen of water. 'I suggest the pair of you get some sleep. Big day tomorrow.'

A yawn escaped Wraith at the mere mention of sleep. She recovered her bedroll from her pack and found a spot not far from Fenrix, Badger, and the campfire. Jaks was close by too.

'Jaks, you still awake?' she asked.

'I am, my dear liberator,' the fiend replied.

'That ability you used on the circlet… could you do the same with a potion?'

'I could certainly give it a try.'

Wraith reached into her cloak and pulled forth the vial of white milky fluid given by the alchemist.

'I was given this by the Guild's Alchemist and told only to use when desperate,' the Slayer said as she handed over the potion.

The sorcerer's eyes flickered and flashed for a moment as she examined the vial before a smile spread across her lips.

'I hate to tease…' Jaks began to say before correcting herself. 'Actually, I love to tease…'

'What is it?' Wraith asked as the fiend's eyes settled and she handed back the potion.

'All I can say is that your alchemist was right,' Jaks said. 'Drink that only when you have no other option.'

'Tease,' Wraith remarked before yawning again.

'I would hate to rob you of the joy of discovery. Now, my dear, I believe it is time we both got some sleep.'

'Thank you,' Wraith said. 'For coming here, I mean. I am glad you are with me… us, I mean.'

'As am I,' the fiend said with a warm smile. 'Sleep now, for tomorrow will bring us more adventure and danger.'

Despite the thoughts of what the coming day would bring, what new horrors awaited them below the fortress, and whether they would find Luthor, no matter what happened to him, exhaustion claimed Wraith, eyes falling heavy and sleep taking hold. With eyes closed, the last she heard was the whistle of arrows in the distance and the thud of impacts, Raven practicing with her bow in isolation once again.

CHAPTER THIRTEEN
THE RUINED FORTRESS OF KARNOCK

A dishevelled body, broken and weak, submerged, and lost in the darkness. A hand rose towards her, words rattling in his throat as he called out.

'Help me... Alena... please...'

'Luthor!' Wraith cried out as she awoke from the nightmare with her heart pounding and sweat streaming from her brow. The hilt of her silver dagger was already in her hand, clutched tight to her chest. Hers was not the only cry though, for another echoed from the darkness. It was still night, the campfires burning and dawn a little while off still. Raven, Quinlan, and Jaks were near, all asleep but for the elf.

'You heard that too?' Wraith asked.

'You and whoever that is in the distance,' Raven replied, rising from her make-shift bed under the stars. Her hands found the bow and quiver of arrows kept close, and both the Slayer and elf waited and watched.

'Perhaps nothing,' Wraith suggested. 'A bird or animal?'

'No...' Raven said as they continued to wait while all others slept.

After what felt like an age, and just as Wraith was about to attempt to sleep again, came a blood-curdling scream of a dying man from beyond the ruins in the darkness to the east.

'That was no animal,' the Slayer warned as she rose to stand. She shook Jaks awake as Raven woke Quinlan. Both quietly warned of the approaching danger.

'Where's Fenrix?' Wraith asked them, the weyre nowhere to be seen.

'On watch,' the fiend replied. 'He relieved me.'

Another, much closer cry of warning sounded out, this time from the north. It sounded once, twice, and a third time before it became a scream silenced with a horrible, gurgling sound. Emerging into view was a man clutching at the tear across his throat, stumbling over the stone remnants of the fortress before falling to the ground. Beyond him, glowing amber eyes watched from the darkness. At first just one pair, but then another and another. Soon, there were a dozen, and then two dozen, eyes all around them.

Wraith looked quickly to the second camp and saw Aederan was up and armed with the dwarven archer, Darsil, the gnome druid, Badger, and the ogre, Axe, at his side. Beyond them was Sir Antonius Lockwood, marshalling his men and followers, barking orders and commands, rallying them into a crude battle order.

'Behind too,' Quinlan warned as he backed away. 'What are they?'

'Wolves,' Raven said as she sniffed the air. A long, loud howl confirmed her suspicions. It was quickly followed by another howl and then more, from all directions.

'Communicating,' Wraith warned.

'Ready to attack.'

The howls died away as one, much louder, feral and monstrous, sounded above all others.

'The Alpha,' Wraith uttered, eyes wide in horror.

The Alpha howled from the darkness again, and one by one, they emerged into the dim light of the campfires and torches. Snarling, with grey and white fur, amber eyes, and blood-stained fangs, they approached slowly, edging towards the camp from all directions. Raven raised her bow, arrow nocked and ready to fly. Quinlan had both his crossbows in hand, and Jaks extended her black wings and raised her spear high, its three points crackling and shining with purple energy. Wraith, with her silver dagger in one hand, drew a pair of her throwing daggers from her cloak with the other.

The wolves slowly advanced, eyeing their prey eagerly as jaws snapped and claws dug at the ground.

'I've never seen so many,' Raven said.

'No one has,' added Jaks.

As one, the wolves stopped fifty paces from the camps. Wraith counted near twenty of the beasts ahead of them, the same behind, and more at their flanks. They waited and watched, like soldiers expecting the order from their commander to attack. Then Wraith saw it, towering over its kin. Powerful body, black fur, red eyes, and a horrid scar across its face, the Alpha approached the dead man and sank its claws into his back. Its fangs then lowered and closed around the guard's head, wrenching it grimly free with one snap of its jaws. It was a beast from nightmares, risen from the shadows.

With blood trickling from its jaws, its red eyes rose to look upon the two camps. Wraith was certain she saw the beast smile before throwing its head back and monstrously howling to the near full-moon above. That was the signal for the wolves' attack.

The beasts roared and howled, leaping forward and charging towards the camps. Arrows and bolts flew from Raven and Quinlan, downing a pair of foes as they closed in. Jaks summoned a storm of ice shards and sent them hurtling out towards their rear, tearing apart one wolf and warding off several others. Wraith waited until the wolves came closer before throwing her daggers. The first flew wide as the wolf ducked away, but the second hit true, imbedding in its throat, killing the beast. Others hurtled over their fallen brethren, Wraith drawing Shatter and roaring in defiance. Raven was with her, loosing another pair of arrows in quick succession before the predators could close the gap.

Wraith threw her silver dagger, forcing the nearest beast away and distracting it long enough for her to dive forward. She slashed Shatter down towards the beast's head, missing, but cutting deep across its back before an arrow punctured its side. Another wolf leapt towards her, and Wraith ducked and rolled away, the deadly claws barely missing. As it landed and turned towards Raven, Wraith was upon it, Shatter stabbing into its flank again and again until it fell.

Quinlan and Jaks fought behind them, defending from the rear and flanks with crossbows, rapier, spear, and the arcane. Raven loosed arrows until her quiver was empty, discarding the bow and drawing her curved daggers. Beyond them, the second camp was a warzone. Sir Antonius led his command in tight formation, cutting down any beast that dared attack. A handful of his followers were dead or dying, one man screaming as he was dragged away into the shadows. Aederan and his group fought nearby, Axe laughing jovially as she brought her namesake down upon the attacking wolves, and Darsil's arrows soared through the night.

As Wraith recovered her silver dagger, she saw shadows move round behind her as a pair of the predators encircled, one ahead and one behind. Their jaws dripped with blood from recent kills, and they snarled, anticipating more blood and death. Their claws dug into the ground and their jaws snapped as they growled.

Me first then, Wraith decided, yelling and charging the wolf in front of her. She took the initiative, hoping the wolf would not expect its surrounded prey to attack. The beast snarled and leapt forward, crashing into the Slayer and sending both tumbling to the ground. Shatter was torn from her grasp and the wolf recovered quickest, bearing down on Wraith with stinking, bloody jaws opening wide. Instinct took hold, and Wraith brought her silver dagger up and into the wolf's open mouth. Its eyes opened wide, and despite the gruesome damage and ruin caused by her blade, the beast continued to attack.

Panicking, Wraith held the silver blade firm with one hand and frantically drew one of her throwing daggers. She stabbed the small blade into the body of the wolf again and again until its legs trembled and collapsed, falling limp on top of her. Wraith struggled to push the dying animal off her just as the second wolf approached. It howled menacingly and slowly advanced as the Slayer fought to free herself. With Wraith's legs still trapped beneath the carcass and her silver blade lodged in the dead wolf's mouth, she swiped her small throwing dagger from side to side in defence. The wolf, sensing an easy kill, leapt forward, but did not reach its target. A whistle sounded in the air before an arrow struck, punching into its back just beneath the neck. The beast stopped and snarled, head rising to search for the new threat. That was its mistake, as a second arrow flew, this one piercing straight through the predator's eye. The wolf swayed for a moment and then collapsed, revealing Darsil in the distance. He and Aederan were coming to them, Wraith and her group, forcing back the wolves. The elf nimbly rushed to Wraith's side and helped her free, both pushing the dead wolf carcass away.

'Come on, Slayer,' Aederan said with an offered hand. 'Plenty more killing to be done this night.'

A new howl echoed across the fortress ruins, forcing all the wolves to stop and look to its source. Wraith and her allies recognised the roar and cheered as they saw Fenrix advance and stalk the Alpha. In his grip was a pair of carcasses, wolves, his axe buried in the head of one. He threw them down before the Alpha in challenge, facing the black-furred beast unarmed. The Alpha roared in reply, monstrous and deafening, charging the weyre. Fenrix thought he was ready, clawed fists raised to strike the beast, but the Alpha was quicker, knocking Fenrix down and savagely biting down onto his shoulder and then his neck. The weyre let out a howl of pain that turned into a roar as his fists struck and connected, colliding with the beast's head repeatedly until the jaws' grip released him. The Alpha's claws dug in deep, carving across Fenrix's chest until he could force it off and back, kicking the mighty wolf away.

Fenrix recovered, breathing deep and bleeding heavily from his wounds. He still faced the Alpha as it paced around him, shaking off the blow to its head and snarling with murderous intent. Its brethren were approaching, ignoring the Forsaken, Aederan's group, and Sir Antonius's command and surrounding the two monsters as they fought. Wraith and her allies rallied, prepared to support Fenrix or defend themselves if the wolves turned and attacked again.

Wraith hurried forwards to his aid, but the nearest wolves turned and growled in warning, forcing her away.

She looked to Raven, but the elf's arrows were spent. Quinlan was recovering from wounds to his arm, blood at his waistcoat and jacket from other injuries. Jaks sat upon the ground, kneeling and breathing deep from exhaustion, a dozen wolf bodies laid out around her. None of them could come to Fenrix's aid.

Fenrix and the Alpha faced each other, staring one another down before the Alpha howled menacingly. It looked Fenrix in the eye, fangs bared and claws hacking at the ground as a beastly growled emanated from its chest. Then the Alpha charged. Fenrix was ready this time. Instead of rising to meet his foe's charge, he took a step back and lifted from the ground a piece of stone debris. Fenrix lifted the stone and thrust it into the Alpha's snapping jaws. The beast was stunned, jaw cracking horribly, but still it raged, hurtling forward and crashing into the weyre. Fenrix was crushed against a fallen fortress wall, pinned and unable to escape as the Alpha's claws slashed across his face. Fenrix pushed the beast's claws away, but its jaws thrust forward and bit deep of his chest and then his neck again, tearing through flesh in bloody ruin.

Fenrix howled with agony at first, blood pouring from his wounds, but then fury took hold. The howl turned into a roar, and with wild eyes, he butted his head forward, colliding with that of the Alpha. The wolf reeled back in a daze before Fenrix's own jaws clamped down on the beast's throat, tearing it open in a feral frenzy. The Alpha staggered back, wounded and suffering, but Fenrix was not down with it yet. The weyre took hold of the wolf, arms wrapping around its neck, tightening, choking, and twisting until tendons, cartilage, and bone snapped. Even then, the Alpha was still trying to fight, biting down on Fenrix's arm and unwilling to let go. Fenrix's fury only grew, his grip loosening for a moment before, with immense strength, he seized the wolf and lifted the beast into the air before bringing the Alpha down upon the stone rubble with a sickening crash once, twice, and then a final third time, the leader of the pack finally dead. Fenrix let out one long howl, scattering the remaining wolves before he too collapsed upon the ruins.

Wraith and the others ran to him, a healing potion already in her hands before she could reach the weyre. She poured its entire contents into his mouth, but even with that, his eyes were closed, breathing shallow and heartbeat slowing. Wraith was about to draw another potion from her cloak before her hand was stopped by the druid, Badger. The gnome spoke in her language, the Slayer not understanding a word, before seeing the druid's hands lower upon the side of Fenrix's head. With a gentle song upon her lips, the gnome stroked his fur, pretty much the only part that was not slick with blood. As she did so, her hands shone with warm light and the wounds on the weyre began to close. Though his eyes were still closed, his chest rose with a long, steady breath. Badger then collapsed beside him, breathing heavy and trembling, pale from the effort.

'I cannot thank you enough,' Wraith said as she supported the gnome. Badger said something back, and though Wraith did not understand it, the gnome's smile was clear enough.

Raven, Quinlan, and Jaks joined them, as did Aederan, and even Sir Antonius. All looked worse for wear, but still standing, still strong.

'He's in good hands,' Aederan reassured as he saw the gnome with Fenrix. 'I think she is quite taken with him.'

'I owe her,' Wraith said. 'The few healing potions I have would not have been enough.'

'Then we can be thankful we all were here when needed.'

'I don't think any of us will be getting much more sleep this night,' Sir Antonius remarked.

'Our guards on watch?' Wraith asked.

'All dead, apart from him,' Aederan replied. 'Thank the Gods he was with us. I don't think any of us could have taken down that Alpha. Not even your sorcerer.'

'Indeed,' Lockwood confessed. 'I had my doubts, but you and your group have certainly proved your worth.'

'High praise indeed,' Quinlan joked.

'Have you even seen wolves in such numbers or with such audacity to attack camps like this?' Raven questioned.

'Never,' Aederan admitted. 'It is most… unnatural.'

'Dark days returned,' Quinlan said, earning a haunted glance from Jaks and several of the others.

'Help me build a fire near him,' Wraith said. 'He's too heavy for us to move, and the least he has earned is some warmth.'

'Double the guards on watch,' Sir Antonius ordered. 'No chances. We have lost far too many this past day.'

All agreed as they looked upon the broken and ruined body of the Alpha.

CHAPTER FOURTEEN
THE RUINED FORTRESS OF KARNOCK

THE LOCKWOOD MAUSOLEUM - EASTERN TOMBS

'You don't need to go down there,' Wraith said as they stood by the embers of the campfire. 'Either of you.'

Neither Raven nor Fenrix acknowledged her words or concern. The elf lifted her wine bottle to her lips but found it empty and dry. She scowled, discarding the bottle before walking past Wraith and the others towards the mausoleum's eastern entrance. She carried her bow still, only a handful of arrows recovered from the night's engagement with the wolves. Few words had been spoken since her flight from the tombs the previous day, but as dawn approached, Raven was with them, ready if not eager to descend into the tombs again and face her fears of the underground. With a flex of her hands, Wraith only hoped for Raven's sake that flames would not prove to be a factor in whatever they faced next.

Fenrix was a different story. He still carried barely healed wounds and fresh scars from the tombs and the brutal fight with the Alpha. He had not woken long ago, thanking Badger for her aid once again. The weyre shared a moment with the druid, heads meeting in gratitude and respect before they parted. Fenrix limped and sighed with pain as he moved, but he too was ready to continue. His wounds had been bandaged with more of the gnome's healing concoctions of moss, weeds, and plants.

'I'm still standing, aren't I?' he responded to Wraith's concern. 'I continue. Where you and the others go, I go.'

The weyre marched past her, axe in hand, but movements slow and careful.

'I'd gladly not go down there,' Quinlan offered with a cheeky smile, the highborn's jacket and waistcoat torn and blood-stained. His wounds had been bandaged and seen to by Badger once the gnome had woken, but the highborn still looked like hell.

'You don't have a choice,' Wraith taunted, pushing him on.

'You couldn't force me away if you tried.' Jaks smiled as she leant close on her spear. The fiend was tired, weakened by the night's exertions on her arcane strength.

As Jaks and Quinlan walked towards the eastern entrance to the crypts below, Wraith cast a look towards their rival's camp. Last night, they were united to survive, but today, they were foes in pursuit of a prize. Sir Antonius Lockwood was barking orders again, his men and those of Aederan's group hurrying to make ready for their own descent. Wraith noticed several were missing from the previous day, losses to the tombs' protection and the wolves in the night.

Aederan turned and looked back, the elf aware he was being watched. He nodded towards Wraith and raised his bare arm, displaying the Guild brand in salute. Wraith did the same, holding up her Guild arrowhead marking. She remembered the silver dagger Aederan had recovered, Luthor's dagger, and wondered again if she would find him amongst the darkness and dangers below.

If you're here, I'm coming, she thought. *Hold on.*

Wraith cast one last look around her camp, checking nothing had been forgotten, before hurrying after her group at the broken and ruined eastern entrance to the mausoleum. There, she found them ready, beaten and bloodied, but unwilling to leave Wraith's side. Fenrix and Quinlan already had torches lit, Raven keeping away from their flames. Fenrix handed his torch to Wraith, his wolf eyes accustomed to the dark.

'We find the Lockwood Lance and we get out of here,' Wraith promised them.

'Even if we haven't found Luthor?' Raven asked quietly.

Wraith paused for a moment before Guildmaster Brevik's rules came to mind.

'Find the Lockwood Lance. No more, no less,' the Slayer said. 'Take all precautions. We know the Lockwood's protected their departed well. I do not want any of us joining the dead down there.'

'I second that,' Quinlan said as he drank from his small flask and then offered it around. Unsurprisingly, no one turned it down, whether for courage or pain relief. The strong-smelling liquid burned Wraith's throat and warmed her stomach. She coughed and gasped as she handed back the flask, earning a moment of laughter from them all.

'It's down there,' Wraith said with a smile on her lips. 'The lance. I know it, and we are the ones who're going to find it.'

'Yes, we are.' Quinlan grinned.

'Shall we?' Jaks gestured, and Wraith paced forwards.

A cracked and broken stone arch made for the eastern entrance to the mausoleum. Names and symbols had been recently etched into the stone by looters, gangs, and thieves. Glass from broken bottles and discarded equipment littered the ground.

'Not a great sign,' Fenrix remarked as they picked their way through the rubble of the fortress and the debris of past explorers.

'We can expect much the same down there,' added Jaks as she struck the butt of her spear against a rock, bright shimmering violet light appearing at her weapon's three points.

'Only one way to know for certain.' Raven pushed her way through and was first to pass under the arch and down the staircase. Wraith followed after a touch of her arrowhead pendant, then Fenrix, Jaks, and lastly Quinlan.

They descended the stairs slowly and carefully, torches and arcane light guiding the way. The staircase itself was marked with more of the graffiti, but then suddenly stopped near the bottom of the stairs. As they stepped down from the staircase, each member of the group heard the sickening, haunting voice of the crypts in their mind again.

'You return,' the voice said. 'I knew you would. You are coming to me, our destinies entwined.'

Wraith, Raven, and Quinlan shuddered, Jaks's eyes and lights upon her spear flickered, and Fenrix growled in warning.

'Guessing you all heard that,' Wraith said.

'I think I left something of importance at our camp,' said Quinlan as he tried to turn back, but Fenrix blocked the way.

'Evil plagues these tombs,' Raven seethed, with arrow already upon bow.

'That might have drawn the giants here,' Jaks suggested. 'And the wolves last night.'

'It was more than hunger,' Fenrix agreed.

'That voice,' Quinlan said. 'You think it's an evil spirit or something? A seraph, or an actual real wraith.'

'It doesn't matter,' the Slayer replied as she stepped forward and away from the staircase. 'We find the Lockwood Lance and get out of here.'

The tombs before them were very similar to what they had discovered the previous day. Stone caskets and urns within the alcoves between pillars, but their condition and state was much worse. All had been opened or overturned, looted, and defiled. Skeletons and bones had been thrown and scattered. Garments, clothes, and tokens of affection torn and trodden. Anything of worth was either long gone or ruined beyond recovery. What was of interest were the bodies of those who were not of the Lockwood bloodline. Thieves, grave-robbers, rogues, and adventurers. Wraith counted near a dozen in sight. As they walked the crypts, keeping watch for any trap or trigger, they inspected the more recently deceased. On many, the flesh was old and rotten, but some were fresher and only days or weeks old.

'Friends of yours?' Raven asked of Quinlan, a tease of the highborn's banditry past.

'No, but perhaps one of yours,' he replied as he inspected one closer; a female dwarf. Upon her arm was the branding of the Guild.

'Uriella,' Raven said with shock. 'I did not even know she had taken this contract.'

'There is another here,' Fenrix warned. 'The brand of the Aelthorn Guild, alike Aederan's band.'

'There are others without markings,' Wraith said. 'A mix of Guild and common rogues.'

'Lockwood's reward has brought many coin seekers,' Jaks remarked.

'And family members,' Wraith said as she made another

discovery. Upon the body of one man, the flesh stripped from his skull and chest, was a wooden shield baring the armoured fist of the Lockwoods. Around his neck too was a locket, also engraved with the family coat-of-arms. He too could have sought out the lance to claim command of the Lockwood family. Wraith opened the locket, revealing a small painted portrait of a young, pretty woman. She thought of taking the locket as a token for Lady Aureilia Lockwood, but then remembered the poor treatment she had given Raven. Instead, she left the dead in peace where they had fallen.

'How did they die?' Jaks asked.

'Spear trap to the gut for this one,' Quinlan said.

'Poison by the stench and bloating of this one.' Raven gagged.

'Caved in skull here,' Wraith said. 'Rival or trap, everyone be careful.'

They advanced through the dark chambers slowly and carefully, caution taken with every step. Jaks's illumination and the light from their torches helped greatly. Raven spotted one trigger around a gathering of urns that launched deadly bolts from the walls. Wraith discovered another, seeing a pattern in the stonework and the dead thieves on the ground. From a distance, she threw a discarded bone onto the slabs and was rewarded with a series of rising spears. Despite the dangers, they progressed until they reached the very end of the chambers. There were no tunnels or doors, no stairways. Nothing. Jaks even tried a spell to reveal passages or hidden routes, but still there was nothing.

'End of the road,' said Quinlan, booting a broken piece of stone away.

'The lance must've been elsewhere,' Wraith conceded. 'Sir Antonius will get his hands on his prize after all.'

'Leaving you empty-handed,' Jaks said with disappointment. 'It was all for nothing.'

'We could always rob Sir Lockwood when he emerges triumphant,' Quinlan suggested with a smirk.

'Of course you'd say that, bandit,' Wraith teased.

'I won't fight Aederan's group,' Fenrix warned. 'I owe them, as I owe you.'

'I wouldn't ask you to,' Wraith assured him. 'If they find the prize first then the reward is theirs. Besides, they have three times our number. Even with a sorcerer on our side, I don't like our chances.'

'Anybody feel that?' Raven asked with a puzzled expression on her face.

'An impending sense of doom?' Quinlan half-joked.

The elf ignored him as she looked to the crypt ceiling and raised a hand. She paced forward and carefully climbed atop one of the tombs, the stone casket easily taking the elf's weight.

'What is it?' Wraith asked.

'A breeze,' Raven replied. 'Ever so slight, but it is here in the depths of this mausoleum, and it is coming from beyond that wall.'

The far wall was faded and lined with cracks, but there was no gap or hole, and certainly nothing that any of their group could see or climb and clamber through. Wraith approached and raised her hand. Raven was right, there was a definitely a gentle breeze coming from beyond that wall. Taking utmost care in case of more lurking traps, the Slayer walked to the wall, hands feeling across the stone and definitely feeling a breeze through the highest small cracks.

'Help me,' she told the others as she pressed against the wall. Jaks, Raven, and Quinlan joined her, pushing against the stone, but it would not budge, not until Fenrix charged the wall. The weyre growled and roared, slamming into the stone once, twice, and then a final third time. The wall tremored with each impact, the cracks growing and deepening, and with the last strike by the weyre a significant portion buckled and came crashing down.

A cloud of dust rose up and engulfed them, extinguishing the aflame torches. All coughed and spluttered, Fenrix breathing heavily from his wounds and efforts in toppling the wall. Jaks struck her spear upon the crypt floor, the three lights at its tips growing stronger, brighter, and illuminating the cavern beyond. The sound of rushing water greeted them from an underground river ahead.

'The search continues,' Wraith said with a growing smile shared by the others.

She clambered through the fallen wall and entered the cavern. Two paths were laid out before them, one that led down to the river, and another that formed a bridge to a tunnel on the far side. Wraith followed the path up to the bridge, but discovered that its centre was gone, fallen and scattered upon the rocks and rushing river below.

'Where now?' Quinlan asked as the others joined the Slayer.

'Through that tunnel,' Wraith said, pointing across the fallen bridge. 'By the looks of it, that river is too fast and deep to cross.'

'What's a river doing under a fortress anyway?' the highborn asked.

'A water source,' Raven replied as she backed up and then ran forward, leaping across the chasm with elven grace and landing on the far side.

'No problem, huh?' Quinlan forced a laugh as he looked across the distance with uncertainty. 'Who's next?'

'Me,' Wraith announced as she ran forward and leapt. Instantly, she knew she would not land on the far side.

Reaching out, she caught the very edge, tumbling down and barely holding on. Raven's hands quickly found the Slayer and dragged her up and onto the far side of the bridge, Wraith falling onto her back as she panted for breath, her heart racing.

'No problem,' she repeated as Raven helped her to her feet.

'Nope. I will pass on this one,' Quinlan said, hands raised in surrender.

'Take him across,' Jaks told Fenrix. The weyre did so, grabbing hold of Quinlan and throwing him over his shoulder before leaping across the fallen bridge with ease.

'Your turn,' Wraith called over to the sorcerer.

Jakseyth instead walked down to the river and held out a hand. The rushing water before her rose up, a frost spreading as it hardened to ice, creating her own bridge. The sorcerer crossed with ease and joined the others with a smile upon her lips.

'You couldn't have done that for all of us?' Quinlan asked.

'Then I wouldn't get to see this look of surprise and admiration on your face,' the fiend said with a soft slap on his cheek. 'Shall we continue?'

They did, entering the tunnel with Fenrix at the lead until the weyre came to an abrupt halt.

'What is it?' Wraith asked, though the question was unnecessary. Ahead of them, the tunnel narrowed and was covered with thick cobwebs on the walls, the ceiling, the floor, and across the tunnel itself. Fenrix was unmoving.

'Spiders, huh?' Wraith asked him.

'Ever since I was a young...' he began to say.

'Pup?' Raven suggested.

'Must've been a lot of them to create webbing as thick

as this,' Jaks said as she inspected the walls. 'Or several big ones.'

'It isn't fresh,' Wraith tried to reassure as she placed a hand to the webs.

'I'd rather you had left me in that cell in Stonemere to rot.' Fenrix grimaced.

'The big bad wolf afraid of a few spiders,' Jaks teased, earning a growl from the weyre. 'Don't worry, I will lead for now.'

The fiend raised her spear, their sole light source high, and advanced into the tunnel, cutting through the webs in their path. Raven, Quinlan, and Wraith followed, Fenrix rooted to the spot before finally snarling in frustration and following. The Forsaken moved slowly and cautiously through the tunnels, care taken with every footstep, weapons held close. Smalls holes covered the floor, walls, and ceiling, like a mass honeycomb in the stone.

Further tunnels led to other routes, some small, some large, some above and below. All were covered in the webbing. Skeletons littered the ground or were hung on the walls and from the ceiling, bound in the webs. Humanoid, animal, and beast cocooned, prey and feed for whatever lurked in the darkness.

'Ah! What's that?' Quinlan suddenly cried out, turning with raised crossbows.

'What?' all of them demanded of the highborn.

'I felt something… I'm sure of it,' Quinlan said fearfully.

'We should leave this damned place,' Fenrix growled.

'It's nothing,' Jaks said. 'Fear takes minds.'

It was then Raven's turn to startle and threaten with raised blades.

'I feel as if something is crawling across my skin,' the elf muttered with shaky words and sweat upon her brow. Wraith placed a hand upon her shoulder, though Raven shrugged it away and pressed on before all stopped as they saw more figures amongst the webbing. Far fresher corpses. There were those that were rotten and stripped of much of their flesh, and others with bodies torn open.

'Other treasure seekers,' Wraith said as she inspected, but did not touch, one halfling carcass. 'This was a Guild member too, by his branding.'

'So was this one,' Quinlan remarked as he looked at a cocooned dwarven female.

'This one was not fed upon,' Raven said as she looked at a dead half-orc. 'His chest and stomach were ripped open from the inside.'

'Hosts,' Wraith realised, remembering the horrible stories she had heard of monsters and beasts of nightmares. She backed away from the corpse, noticing her footsteps were tougher as the webbing pulled at her boots.

'Wait… wait,' Jaks said as she hurried forward. The sorcerer came to a sudden stop at one. 'This man, yes, he was of Lockwood's command. I'd recognise that ugly face anywhere.'

'Hey, mage,' Quinlan said as he looked above them all. 'Isn't that the red-skinned fiend you disliked so much?'

The group looked up to the tunnel above them where a dozen bodies wrapped tight hung from thick lines of web like rope. Sure enough, among them was the red-skinned fiend Skiminos. Alongside him were other cocoons; Darsil the dwarf, Badger the gnomish druid, and Mason the young squire. All were tightly bound and hanging above them, silent and barely moving but for their eyes. Their eyes were open wide in shock, terror, and warning.

'They're alive,' Wraith said with horror.

'Cut them down!' Fenrix roared upon seeing the gnome who had helped his injuries.

'Aederan,' Raven said as she spotted the elf higher than the others and raised her bow. 'Fenrix, catch them.'

'Wait, don't...' Jaks tried to warn them, but it was too late. Raven loosed an arrow, severing the web that held Aederan and sending his cocoon tumbling down. The elf loosed two more arrows as Quinlan fired his bolts, freeing all those they recognised and sending them falling to the ground, where Fenrix waited to catch them and cut them free of the cocoons.

It was then that they heard the skittering. The dreadful, creeping sound echoed from ahead of them, behind them, above, and below. The terrible sound grew in volume as it closed in around them.

'Get out of here!' Aederan cried once his face was freed. 'Save yourselves!'

CHAPTER FIFTEEN
THE RUINED FORTRESS OF KARNOCK

THE LOCKWOOD MAUSOLEUM – THE NEST

Wraith looked back the way they came, and to her horror, saw a towering eight-legged creature of nightmares approach. Eight unblinking eyes stared at the Forsaken and the freed captives, jaws twitching as they oozed with poison. Its black and green body shuddered for a moment before its jaws opened wide and unleashed a horrid, deafening shriek. At once, the honeycomb of holes and tunnels erupted, spiders of all shapes and sizes emerging and skittering towards the intruders.

'Get them free and on their feet!' Wraith ordered as she slammed the silver dagger into the body of a leaping spider the size of her fist. 'Now!'

Quinlan fired his crossbow bolts and backed away as two spiders leapt onto his chest, and another crept up his leg. Fenrix roared in fear and fury, smashing any that neared with clawed fists and axe. Jaks unleashed a freezing cloud ahead of them, encasing dozens of arachnids in ice, many shattering to pieces. Raven cut the captives free, handing Aederan a curved dagger and Darsil her bow as she set to free the gnome, fiend, and squire.

'We cannot go back!' Wraith warned as the ache in her hands grew tremendously. She crushed one of the smaller spiders against the wall with her boot and then stabbed Shatter through the abdomen of one the size of a dog. The creature's body burst open as hundreds of tiny spider babies tore free.

'Where is the rest of your group?' Wraith called to Aederan as the elf fought beside his rescuers. 'Where is Sir Antonius?'

'Farther ahead,' the elf replied as he swung his borrowed blade with hatred. 'Our comrades could be fighting still if they are not with us!'

'We can't stay here!' Quinlan warned as giant spiders continued to emerge from all around them. One hideous red and green arachnid spat fluid from its jaw, barely missing the highborn, who dove away and then swung his rapier blade up, slicing off legs and pincers. The wall and stone the fluid touched hissed and burned, the stone melted by the acidic venom.

Wraith agreed, for back the way they came, the towering spider continued to slowly approach.

'Jaks!' the Slayer called out. 'Push forward!'

With shimmering eyes and a flash of the arcane, Jaks pushed the ice cloud forward, freezing more of the arachnids and clearing the way. Still the spiders tried to emerge from the holes and cracks in the tunnels, the fiend's razor-sharp wings slashing at any that escaped her frost.

'This way!' the mage cried as she, Aederan, and Fenrix charged on, the frost crunching under their boots and frozen spiders were smashed aside by the weyre. Raven and Quinlan followed, leading Badger, Mason, and Skiminos as Wraith and Darsil brought up the rear.

'*You march willingly towards her?*' the haunting voice asked within each of their minds. '*Brave, but foolish.*'

'Shut up!' Raven screamed back as they ran on, the infestation continuing all around them, spiders emerging from the holes and cracks in the walls, ceiling, and floors. The group hurried, pace quickening as the horrid shrieks of the arachnids echoed down the tunnels.

'I never thought I would thank one of your kind,' Skiminos muttered to Jaks, 'but you have it, regardless! These foul creatures are abominations!'

'I'd have thought you'd be quite at home amongst the vermin, Scharbaxian!' the mage replied. 'How were you all trapped in such a way?'

'You will see soon enough!' Skimonos hissed, baring his fangs.

They hurried on until, at last, they emerged at the edge of a vast cavern. The ground, walls, and high ceiling were covered in more of the honeycomb of holes, all covered in webs. Fallen torches lit the cavern, and weaponry littered the floor amongst several dead, likely from Sir Antonius and Aederan's group. Upon the walls close by were two of Lockwood's command, cocooned, hundreds of similar bodies of long deceased enveloped in webs upon the walls. Through the webbing, the chests and stomachs of the two still living captives appeared expanded and bloated.

The spiders behind Wraith and her group continued to pursue, hundreds of them, including the largest towering arachnid. As they neared, Jaks turned to face them, eyes shimmering as her raised hand shone. A flickering barrier erupted from her palm, a shield, blocking the tunnel and holding back the horde. The largest slammed its body into the barrier, but it held firm.

A horrid shriek drew all eyes but Jaks's to the very

centre of the vast cavern, all silent and still at the sight of a nightmare given life.

A man, one of Lockwood's thugs, screamed as he was dragged to the centre of the cavern, where the biggest arachnid, as tall as two men, with a green and crimson body and legs lined with barbed spikes, bulbous abdomen and fangs dripping with venom and blood, waited. *The queen,* Wraith realised. Two smaller spiders the size of dogs dragged the man, his body barely moving but for his cries, likely paralysed by a venom. He was thrown before the queen, where all he could do was scream and cry as the monstrous pincers wrapped around him, his head lost amongst the jaws. His cries became a gargled grunt, and then silence until the queen released him. The man's body was now gaunt and greyed, barely skin and bones.

'It drained him,' Wraith uttered with horror.

The man's body was discarded, thrown aside by the queen, where it landed amongst a dozen skeletons and at least three more of Lockwood's command. The knight himself, the ogre known as Axe, the squire Petero, and many others were pinned down by a horde of the spiders on the far side of the cavern, awaiting their turn for an audience with the queen.

'Free those two men,' Wraith ordered. 'Quickly and quietly. All of you, arm yourselves. When ready, half of us will attack the queen whilst the rest free Lockwood and the others. Jaks, how long can you hold them off?'

'Not indefinitely,' the fiend said through gritted teeth from the effort as the spiders continued to attack the barrier, the largest still slamming its legs and body against the shield. 'They will find another way if my spell does not fall.'

'I know, but hold as long as you can,' Wraith asked of

the sorcerer. 'Together, with everyone, we may be able to force them back so we can escape this place.'

Aederan, Darsil, Badger, and Skiminos armed themselves with whatever was near, only the squire, Mason, staying back. The young boy looked terrified, even more so when Wraith forced the hilt of one of her daggers into his hand.

'Stay behind us,' she said in an attempt to comfort him. 'And don't accidentally stab us.'

He smiled for a moment before all looked on in fear as the two captives held on the walls were freed, and both screamed out. Though freed, the halfling and elven male fell to the ground, both writhing and clutching at their swollen bodies.

'Keep them silent,' Wraith ordered as quietly as she could, fearful of discovery.

Raven and Quinlan tried to hush and comfort the pair, but quickly realised their cries were not of fear. Their bodies, chests, and stomachs shuddered, something moving beneath the flesh. The skin began to tear, and their screams only grew louder.

'Back away,' Wraith ordered as she remembered the corpses they had seen in the tunnel.

The victims fell silent as their bodies tore open in a grotesque display of gore. Bones and organs were torn free as hundreds and thousands of tiny spiders burst free.

'Stay back,' Raven warned as the swarm scattered into the honeycomb of holes in the ground. Then came the sound of discovery that Wraith and all around her had been dreading; the queen's shriek shaking the cavern. Pain flared in Wraith's hands as the echoing replies of thousands of spiders sounded in all directions.

'Raven, protect Jaks and the squire,' Wraith ordered,

seeing the elf armed with her bow once again. 'Aederan, circle round and free your people. Meet us at the centre.'

'On it,' the elf replied, as he led Darsil and Badger away.

'I will stay and protect my kin,' Skiminos said as he looked to Jaks. The red-skinned fiend had armed himself with a pair of curved blades, scimitars.

Jaks looked to argue at first before relenting and nodding in agreement, her tail curling up before impaling a small spider on the wall behind her.

'What of us?' Quinlan nervously asked.

'You, me, and Fenrix... we're the distraction,' Wraith warned.

'We will take the queen?' Fenrix asked, his own axe and a second found amongst the dead raised high in rage.

'Go!' Wraith urged them, already seeing that more of the giant spiders were gathering around their queen.

Wraith, Fenrix, and Quinlan ran on, cutting down giant spiders as they rose up from the ground. Others descended from the cavern ceiling down long strands of silk like ropes, reaching out with long, twitching legs as they fell. Wraith carved through them, Shatter and her silver dagger coated in gore. Quinlan repeatedly switched between his crossbow with one hand and his rapier blade in the other as they pushed on towards the queen. Fenrix roared and charged forward, spearheading the way as he tore a route through the hordes of spiders uniting to defend their queen.

Ahead, Wraith could see Aederan and his group had circled round the cavern and reached Lockwood's bound group. Wraith's threat to the queen had drawn a significant number of the spiders away, and Darsil's arrows made quick work of any remaining. Already, Aederan and his companions were working on freeing the knight and his company, and Wraith hoped they would join them soon and not take the chance to flee. She could not think of that, not now the hordes and their queen bared down on her.

The queen saw the coming threat and rose to meet it, shrieking and displaying her fearsome jaws and rows of fangs. Fenrix roared back and leapt at the towering arachnid, bringing both axes down upon a leg and near severing it. The towering spider screamed but did not flee, instead lunging at the weyre and biting down on his back and thigh. Fenrix was thrown back, and Wraith saw that already his eyes and veins beneath the fur were darkening with venom. The queen moved to attack again but was forced back as Quinlan fired a crossbow bolt straight into one of her many black eyes.

Wraith fought her way towards Fenrix, thoughts on the antidote in her cloak that she prayed could combat the spider's toxin. The weyre urged her away though as he coughed, roared, and then coughed again, retching horribly a foul dark liquid to the cavern floor. As he did so, his eyes and veins recovered, the spider's venom purged.

'This curse would never let my suffering be ended by a mere spider bite!' he said. 'Now I kill my fear of these wretched things!'

Cheers sounded throughout the cavern, and a smile grew across Wraith's lips as she saw Sir Antonius and Aederan fighting their way through the spider hordes, edging towards the centre of the cavern where Wraith, Fenrix, and Quinlan fought alone.

As Wraith moved to join Quinlan's side, she felt fingers wrap around her ankle and the grip tighten, pulling hard and tripping her over. Wraith looked down in horror as she saw that the thing that gripped her leg was the frail corpse of a man that had been drained of life by the queen spider. The Slayer recognised the thing from her studies, an undead ghoul, a corpse devoid of soul. With greyed, lifeless eyes and pale, milky flesh, he groaned inhumanly as he clawed at his prey and sought to bite down on her flesh. Wraith replied with a boot kicked hard in the ghoul's face again and again, destroying the bone of its skull until it finally released her. As she scrambled to her feet, she saw the other corpses, more than a dozen of them, begin to shudder and rise, awoken by the arrival of life and living flesh.

'Cast down these abominations!' Sir Antonius commanded as the knight and his hired force charged across the cavern and tore through the spiders and rising ghouls. They fought like beasts, roaring and snarling, killing anything in their path, the fear of defeat, captivity, and facing death released and fuelling their rage. In the centre of the cavern, the tide was turning, and the spiders were being driven back, Wraith, Aederan, and Lockwood's groups surrounding the mighty spider queen.

'Wraith!' a scream shouted out from the far side of the cavern, and the Slayer turned in time to see Jak's barrier crack and then shatter. The sorcerer, Raven, Skiminos, and the squire were thrown back as a horde of spiders burst into the cavern, the largest towering beast at their lead. It was smaller than the queen, but still much bigger than anything else in the cavern. *The king,* Wraith named it. Jaks, Raven, Skiminos, and Mason were lost amongst the chaos, for Wraith could only focus on the threats around her and the looming spider king thundering forward to defend its queen. The king stabbed a leg down and pinned one of Lockwood's thugs before biting through the torso of another. One man threw a spear at the monster, striking its body, but his reward was the king's attention. The spider pounced on him and wrapped its jaws around his neck that then snapped shut, the man's head freed of his body and bouncing to the ground. Seeing Wraith and others so near to its queen, the arachnid rose up and unleashed a torrent of silk webs. Wraith was closest and was thrown down and pinned to the ground, half-encased in the webbing. She pulled against it, hair and skin tearing and drawing a cry of agony from her lips. She tried to reach up for her cloak, for her daggers, the potions and vials, anything, but she was utterly trapped and defenceless.

Fenrix dived away from the torrent of webbing, but his arm was struck and restrained to his body. More webbing hit the weyre, pinning his legs to the ground. Fenrix roared as he struggled to fight free, clawing at the webbing with his free hand in desperation as more spiders threatened.

A dwarf charged to Wraith's aid with a raised sword, but the spider rose to face him. From its jaws, it spat a torrent of acid, covering the dwarf and melting flesh and bone. Her would-be saviour screamed once before his face and skull were dissolved, the dwarf dead within moments. Lockwood, Aederan, and their followers fought on against the towering spider king and its army as the arachnids threatened to overwhelm them again. Back on the far side of the cavern, Raven, Skiminos, and Jaks fought back to back, surrounded, with the young squire hiding between them.

That left only Quinlan facing the queen and the ghouls rising from the pile of bodies near. Greatly outnumbered, the highborn secured his crossbows within his jacket and drew his rapier blade. Surprisingly, he showed no fear. With a swift movement, he dived away from the reaching legs of the queen and cut through the body of a shambling ghoul. Another stumbled towards him, rotted mouth open in a guttural roar before the highborn's blade tore through it.

Quinlan then turned on the queen with a raised sword,

but he did not see the spiders descending from the cavern ceiling. One landed on his back and then another at his shoulder, making him stumble and struggle for balance. The arachnids bit at him as more landed, five upon him, until finally, he was forced to his knees before the queen. The largest of the spiders reached down towards him and buried two fangs into his chest, drawing a cry from the highborn that was heard by all as his rapier fell from his grasp.

Wraith fought against the webbing, trying to summon the flames at her hands, but nothing happened, not even an ember for the ache was gone. Fenrix roared as he tore himself free of the webs with feral rage, but a dozen giant spiders were already upon him and forcing him back. Sir Antonius and his men were struggling just to survive, as was Aederan's party. An elven arrow soared across the cavern, but one of the spiders leapt up to save its queen, taking the shaft to its own body.

Quinlan, in the grips of the queen, was dragged closer, her jaws opening wide and wrapping around his head. He did not moan or cry in fear but yelled a war-cry as he faced his horrific end, raising his hands up and into the jaws.

The queen then shuddered, head trembling before it shuddered again as one of its big black eyes burst open. Quinlan was dropped as the queen stumbled backwards, body quivering as it screamed, crashing to the floor. Its legs curled up underneath its body before the queen fell silent and still, dead.

All, even the spiders, looked on in complete shock and surprise as Quinlan rose up with a crossbow in each hand.

'And people ask why I carry two,' he said with pride.

A great mummer rippled amongst the hordes of spiders as by their hundreds they fled, skittering down the many tunnels and holes in all directions. Only the king and the few still moving ghouls remained. Lockwood's group encircled the towering arachnid as Aederan's group slew the last of the ghouls. Fenrix hurried to Wraith's aid, cutting through the webs with his axe and freeing her as Raven and Jaks returned to them, Mason still remaining close. Skiminos was with them too, a bloody gash across his chest, but the fiend was grinning with pride as he twirled his gore-covered scimitars through the air.

'I can't move,' Wraith said with horror as she realised she could not lift her hands, arms, or legs.

'You've been bitten,' Raven said as she spotted bite marks on her neck and leg. Wraith had barely noticed the wounds, but the paralysing venom had taken effect whilst she was trapped in the web.

Raven pulled open Wraith's cloak and found the pockets where her potions and vials were secured. She quickly pulled out the remaining antidote and poured it into her mouth. The potion tasted horrible, like rotten fish, but it worked quickly, her fingers instantly prickling and loosening. With her allies defending her, she could only watch as Lockwood led his command in defeating the king spider. The giant spider was impaled with arrows, crossbow bolts, and spears, but still it fought until Axe crushed another leg with a warhammer and forced the beast to the ground. It was Lockwood who climbed onto the monster's back and stabbed down with his broadsword through its skull, ending the arachnid's life.

As Wraith was helped to her feet by Fenrix and Raven, she saw the last of the spiders panic and flee. The battle was over, for now, and the nest had fallen quiet. Wraith received a nod of appreciation from Sir Antonius, though no words were uttered.

'Not even a thank you.' Jaks chuckled with disbelief. The sorcerer was tired, breathing heavily, and covered in sweat. Her use of the arcane had exhausted her, but still the fiend smiled.

'You have my thanks,' Aederan replied. 'My lot would all be spider feed if it weren't for you.'

'I hope you'd have done the same if it was the other way round,' Wraith said as the feeling returned to her legs and arms and she tried to stand by herself. Raven continued to support her for the moment, seeing the Slayer struggle to balance.

Quinlan was on the ground before the spider queen, pale, but with a smile on his face. Badger was already seeing to the two puncture wounds at his chest from the queen's fangs, the highborn's waistcoat and shirt stained with blood.

'Did you see me?' he asked as Wraith and the others approached. 'I took down this massive… thing! The biggest one… me!'

'We saw it,' Wraith said, unable to hide a smile and pride in the former-bandit.

'You shouldn't have been able to move after those fangs bit you,' Jaks said. 'The poison should have paralysed your entire body in an instant.'

'I do live a charmed life.' He sniggered.

'The antidote I gave you after the manticore's sting,' Wraith said. 'It must still be in your blood.'

'Strong stuff, that,' Raven commented.

'Thank the Gods,' Quinlan replied, still grinning. 'Oh, the tales I have to tell now. I killed the biggest beastie. Me, Quinlan Vespasian Clysley the Fourth!'

'But not without loss,' Wraith said as she picked up his two fallen crossbows. One was covered in spider-gore but still functional, but the other was damaged, the limb cracked and bent back with string hanging loose.

'No, no, no, no, no,' the highborn muttered as he

quickly seized his prized weapons and inspected the damage.

'Can it be repaired?' Wraith asked.

'I hope so,' Quinlan answered with disappointment before securing the broken crossbow in his pack and then rigorously attempting to clean the second crossbow.

'Now what do we do?' Raven asked as she took Quinlan's flask from his pocket and drank deep.

'I don't know about the rest of you, but I want to get the hell out of here,' Fenrix snarled.

Wraith was about to reply, but the haunting voice returned to their minds first.

'*Now you have slain her, you have proven your worth. Come to me, for I have what you seek.*'

'You have the lance?' Sir Antonius demanded. 'Show yourself, damn it! I have had it with your taunts!'

No reply came, much to the knight's endless frustration.

'We continue,' he finally decided. 'We are close. We have to be.'

'Two score of your group lay dead around you,' Wraith said. 'Is the lance really worth your life?'

'They knew what they signed on for,' the knight sneered. 'I have lost a lot of manpower in this endeavour. A lot of coin. Too much to turn back now. I must seize the lance and unite my family. It is worth the cost we have paid. We will return to the crypts and to our search. Nothing has changed.'

'You have no idea what that voice is,' the Slayer continued, undaunted by Lockwood's misgivings, 'nor what it wants.'

'I only care for what I want. What I need,' Lockwood argued further. 'If you want to retreat, then be my guest.'

'Your payment is not worth all this,' Skiminos warned

with bloodied scimitars in hand. 'I should leave now before I too fall to this madness.'

'Oath-breaker, are you?' the knight asked.

'Better an oath-breaker than dead,' the fiend replied. 'Besides, who will speak of my cowardice once you are lost to these tombs as well?'

'For once, I agree with him,' Jaks said, impressed with her distant brethren.

'The shares of the dead,' Sir Antonius said after hasty contemplation, 'remain at my side, and they will be evenly distributed between you.'

'Double shares,' Skiminos argued.

'Of course, greed prevails,' Jaks mocked.

'So be it,' the knight said with a grin. 'This task is almost over, my friend. We will seize the lance and all the glory that comes with it.'

The knight marched away, barking orders at his squires, Petero and Mason, leaving the red-skinned fiend to contemplate whether he had made the right choice.

'And you?' Wraith asked of Aederan before seeing that the assassin was being hugged tightly by Axe, rejoicing in the reunion of their still intact group. The elf had been lifted off his feet with arms pinned to his body by the tight embrace.

'Put me down, Axe,' the elf encouraged.

'Axe no more,' the female ogre said as she lifted the warhammer still stained with spider guts high. 'Name now Hammer.'

'What now for you?' Wraith repeated so that Aederan could hear.

'Our contract has not ended,' the elf said with a raised voice so that his employer could hear. 'But perhaps we could work together. We have lost half our strength and would welcome additional blades with us. There was another route we could still take and search within these crypts. We only came down this way because of a scattering of golden coins and jewels that led us here.'

'A trap,' Wraith said. 'Clever bugs.'

'So it would appear,' Aederan replied. 'Join with us and let us see this contract fulfilled.'

'First to find the lance still the rule?' Wraith asked, earning a nod from Aederan.

'And don't forget our wager,' Darsil grunted as he recovered arrows from the spider carcasses.

'As long as you do not get in our way,' Lockwood called to them, having heard the discussions. 'And we find the lance first, you may come with us.'

'Help me... Alena... please...'

She heard it again, Luthor's voice in her head. She looked to those around her, but none showed any sign that they had heard what she had.

Wraith looked back to her group, to the recovering Raven, Jaks, Quinlan, and Fenrix. All were tired, all were hurting, but none of them wanted to give up.

'I cannot turn back,' she said. 'Limso's challenge remains and the contract is unfinished. I must go on, but…'

'We've come this far,' Raven interrupted. 'We should see this to its end.'

'The worst is over. It has to be,' Fenrix said with happiness as he kicked a spider carcass.

'I killed that thing,' Quinlan said proudly as he pointed to the queen spider. 'Any reward for it?'

'Two puncture wounds in your chest,' Raven said as she patted him on the back.

'I am with you,' said Jaks lastly to Wraith with a warm smile. 'Always.'

'Then we continue,' Wraith said, though her voice was far from certain. Luthor's pleas still echoed in her mind.

Fenrix growled, bringing both his axes down on a nearby spider again and again in a frenzied rage. The weyre finally stopped, panting hard from the effort, and looked up to see everyone in the cavern watching him.

'What?' Fenrix grumbled. 'Its legs twitched.'

CHAPTER SIXTEEN
THE RUINED FORTRESS OF KARNOCK

THE LOCKWOOD MAUSOLEUM – THE DEEPEST TOMBS

Exhausted and aching, the members of the Forsaken followed Sir Antonius Lockwood and his command through the tunnels. All were silent as they paced through the tunnels, wary of any sound or sign of danger, or simply too exhausted for conversation. Wraith moved sluggishly, her body still fighting the spider's paralysing toxins. Jaks breathed heavily and leant on her spear for support, drained by her use of the arcane. Raven was still wide-eyed and shaken, fearful of the enclosed surroundings of the tombs and the dangers they held. Only three arrows remained in her quiver, but the elf's curved knives, still dripping with arachnid gore, were held tightly in her grasp. Fenrix limped heavily as he walked, wounds from the previous night against the wolves still troubling him, let alone those suffered against the arachnids. Quinlan followed, still proud of his victory over the spider queen, but saddened at the loss of one of his ancestral crossbows.

Under their feet were handfuls of scattered coins, the treasure used to lure Sir Antonius Lockwood's followers into the spiders' den. From a command that had numbered more than thirty, the knight's men had been reduced down to a red-skinned fiend, a gnome, a female dwarf, three human thugs, and his two squires. Aederan and his group were still with them, though the elf had lost near all the confidence and charm the assassin had so readily displayed before. Darsil, Badger, and the newly named Hammer followed on dutifully, but it was clear to see none of them wanted to dwell in the mausoleum any longer. Aederan was bound by the same vow as Wraith, a Guild contract taken. They could not leave until the contract was complete and one of them had reclaimed the Lockwood Lance. Sir Antonius was more driven than ever, angered at their failures so far and taunted by the voice that spoke in each of their heads.

The cavern tunnels led back to the crypts, those already explored by Sir Lockwood's expedition, much like those Wraith and her Forsaken had already explored. Tombs, stone caskets, and statues honouring the dead, all had been searched without sign of the lance.

'I told you we should not have gone down there,' Aederan said to his employer as they returned to the crypt.

'We leave no stone unturned,' Sir Antonius said. 'We press on to claim what is rightfully mine.'

'This way,' Skiminos said with scimitars still drawn and pointing ahead. 'There is a staircase that will take us farther. It is the only path that remains to us.'

'A further descent into the darkness,' Quinlan muttered, instantly regretting his words as he saw Raven shudder and grimace.

'We near the prize,' Sir Antonius declared. 'It will soon

be in my grasp, and you all will receive your share of the riches.'

The knight's misguided attempt at inspiring failed miserably, garnering only grimaces and utterings of distaste.

'Stay close,' Wraith warned her own followers. 'We have come too far to lose each other now.'

None spoke, but all understood. The fiend sorcerer, the cursed wolf, the disgraced highborn, the shunned elf, and the nameless Slayer. They marched towards the stone staircase together.

The moment Wraith took her first step onto the stairs, she heard it. Luthor's voice in her head. It felt different this time though; closer and more desperate.

'Hurry, Alena. Please help me...'

'I'm coming,' Wraith replied under her breath.

'Yes, you are, aren't you?' The haunting voice returned, heard by all by the expressions of shock and horror on their faces. *'Every step brings you closer to me. Every step brings you closer to the lance.'*

'It will be mine!' yelled back Sir Antonius.

'Come and claim it,' the voice jeered. *'I have longed to meet one of the descendants and judge their worth. Come. Submit yourself for judgement.'*

'You will die by my sword, spectre!' the knight vowed as he pushed his way forward and hurried down the staircase, all others forced to hurry after him until they reached the lowest chambers of the Lockwood Mausoleum, stepping over the scattered remnants of what had been mighty stone doors.

To keep something out, or perhaps something trapped inside, Wraith wondered as she held her torch close to the doors.

'Here resides... Lord... Lavenell... Lockwood,' she read. 'This is it. This is where the viscount told us the

Lance would be. This has to be it. The Lance must be here.'

Though the discovery should have filled them with cheer and hope, the path ahead utterly dismayed. The darkness of those crypts was near all consuming. The handful of torches and the light of Jaks' spear could scarce penetrate the gloom. Wraith's eyes, though trained by the Guild, could barely make out their surroundings without the flames of a torch held close, her own hand lost when held at arm's length.

Around them were stone caskets and tombs similar to those encountered above, but these had not been disturbed by thieves and grave-robbers. They had been desecrated and ripped apart. Statues whose features were lost to time had been toppled and shattered. Urns were smashed and their contents scattered. Rage and fury had taken this place. Skeletons had been dragged from their caskets and thrown to the ground, warriors still wearing the armour they fought and died in now discarded and cast aside.

'Somebody was angry,' Fenrix grunted with the same suspicions.

Wraith did not like the darkness, nor the destruction around them. She pulled one of the acid vials from her cloak and poured its contents over the blade of Shatter. The shortsword was undamaged by the corrosive fluid, but any flesh and bone it touched would burn.

'Search for the lance,' Sir Antonius ordered. 'It has to be here.'

There were tokens of value that remained; gold, jewels, weaponry, and armaments. None had been plundered, and in the dim light, many items found their way into the pockets of the intruders. Wraith saw several coins and a jewel or two disappear into Quinlan's pockets as Fenrix admired an aged halberd, and Raven raised a pair of gauntlets to the dim light. Wraith cared little for the riches and treasures as she peered into the darkness of the crypt ahead of them. Jaks was beside her, the mage clutching her spear with eyes closed and breathing slow.

'This is the resting place of the heroes who felled the sorcerer Zarakahn,' Jaks whispered. 'This is the most sacred site of rest in all the mausoleum, yet… something is wrong.'

'This place is as much a ruin as the rest of the citadel,' Wraith replied, though she heard the concern and possibly even fear in the fiend's voice. 'What is it?'

'I… I do not know. I…' Jaks said before her eyes suddenly snapped open with terror. 'We are not alone here.'

Badger took a step ahead of them into the darkness, but stopped as a cascade of fearful words erupted from the gnome druid. Aederan stepped beside Wraith and Jaks, the elf trying to calm his compatriot until he too looked on in terror.

'What does she say?' Wraith asked.

'No…' Aederan stammered. 'It cannot be…'

'*At long last, I bid you welcome,*' the haunting voice called, though this time the voice was deafening, overwhelming in its closeness. More words were uttered, a chant in a language Wraith did not recognise.

A bell chimed in the distance followed by a chorus of screams, unnerving all who stood in the darkness of the chamber.

'No…' Jaks uttered in fear. 'No, not this…'

The bell struck again, and the screams echoed closer and from all directions this time.

'Don't listen!' Jaks pleaded. 'Whatever you hear, do not listen! All of you, fight it!'

'*Join me,*' called the voice.

One last time, the bell struck before the screams sounded as if emanating from within Wraith herself. The pain struck like claws tearing into her skull, impaling her mind. Her senses were lost, sight and sound taken, cast adrift from the physical and torn from the tombs of the Lockwoods.

Wraith found herself upon the battlements of Arnhold Castle, but a girl once again. Snow drifted in the air as the sun shone above. People walked the courtyard below, happy and cheerful, nothing amiss. The arrowhead banner of the Athscar family flew high.

'This was your home, wasn't it?' a man called to her as he approached along the battlements. He was young and strong, with soft green eyes and a smile upon his face. He was draped in simple robes and approached with empty hands raised.

'This was all taken from you long ago,' the man said, 'amidst a night of blood and snow.'

'My family,' Wraith said in shock.

'I am sorry for your losses.' A warm smile crept across his lips, and he nodded at something behind Wraith. She turned and stood aghast, eyes welling with tears in an instant. Ahead of her stood the people she knew once as her family; her father and mother, older brothers, and younger sister. They all appeared as they had the last time Wraith had seen them. Happy, healthy, and together.

'Alena,' they called to her, a name she had almost forgotten.

Wraith's eyes were drawn to one of them, the youngest, a girl with a beaming smile and hair tied in pigtails. Memories came rushing back of games, play, laughter, and fun. The little girl was both her sister and best friend, though after so long she struggled to remember her name until it suddenly returned to mind. *Ellowyn.*

'Elly,' Wraith whispered with a smile breaking across her lips.

She took one step, then another, and then more as she ran towards her family, tears streaming down her cheeks. Happiness overwhelmed her, but then the memory of that night, of her father held aloft in execution, returned to her mind.

'No. No, I lost you. I lost all of you,' Wraith said as she forced herself to stop and fresh tears fell. These were not of joy, but of deep and terrible guilt. 'It was my fault. It was all my fault. I brought death to us. I brought ruin to our family. My secret tore us apart. I am so sorry.'

'The pain you feel needs taunt you no longer,' the man called to Wraith. 'All this can be returned to you. All that pain, all that sorrow. It can be erased.'

'You can do that?' Wraith asked.

'We can do that, my dear girl. Together, we can achieve a great many wonders. I can feel it. You and I, we are as one. I feel the power within you that has been hidden so long. It was the secret that cast such terrible ruin upon all you loved. It need not be such a burden.'

'Who are you?'

'You know the answer to that already,' he replied as he stood near and placed a comforting hand upon her shoulder.

'Zarakahn,' she realised, the sorcerer of legend.

'It gladdens the heart to know that I am still remembered,' he said warmly. 'I have been imprisoned within the grounds of Karnock for far too long. Help me. Free me, and together we can return all you have lost.'

Wraith looked at her parents, at her brothers and sister. They urged her closer, smiles and laughter upon their lips. Wraith could feel their love, the love she had missed for so many lonely years. She could not help but ask herself that if there was a chance that they could be returned, was she a fool not to take it?

'I... I...' she began to say, words a struggle as emotions overwhelmed her. Just as she was about to accept, one last distant voice reached out.

'Alena... don't. Please, don't...'

'Luthor...' she uttered.

'Ignore the cretin,' Zarakahn said dismissively.

'Cretin?' Wraith questioned as a flare of rage erupted from within. 'He is here?'

'He does not matter,' the sorcerer said with growing irritation. 'He has been valuable, I admit, but now you are here, I have no use for him. My focus is you, and you have a choice, dear girl. Make it now. Seize what you have always wanted or suffer the same fate as Luthor and all your pathetic friends.'

'Pathetic?' Wraith as the rage within grew into a fire. 'You are wrong, Zarakahn. We are Forsaken.'

In her hand appeared her blade, Shatter, and she turned and thrust the shortsword into the sorcerer's chest. No blood flowed from the wound, but Zarakahn's body shuddered, and the sorcerer looked on in utter shock. His skin aged and lined with wrinkles as his hair whitened and fell from his scalp. His eyes sank into his skull and then vanished as the skin and flesh faded further until only bone remained.

'Then I shall take from you what I desire,' the skull of Zarakahn swore as Arnhold Castle, Wraith's home, flickered and faded from view as the darkness of the Lockwood Mausoleum claimed her once again.

Wraith fell to the stone floor of the crypt, gasping for air. All around her, the others were likewise afflicted, stricken and fallen. Raven and Quinlan struggled to recover as Fenrix snarled angrily. Jaks reached out and took Slayer's hand in her own.

'It is Zarakahn,' Wraith warned. 'The sorcerer is still here.'

'It is far worse,' Jaks replied as she still looked on in terror.

The chamber that had been so utterly purged of light before suddenly illuminated as green flames erupted from torches upon the walls. Wraith was forced to cover her eyes until they attuned and she could take in the true horror around her.

She saw that the crypt was one large, circular chamber, bodies impaled and hanging from the walls. The ground was covered in more bones and skeletons, more of the desecrated dead, but it was what waited in the centre of the room that truly terrified her. A gaunt, skeletal body Wraith recognised as Zarakahn sat upon a throne of skulls, and with green, glowing eyes, stared back at the intruders from beneath a dark hood. What once were fine robes were now torn and tarnished, likely the very clothing worn when the sorcerer fell to the Lockwood Lance. A cloak of dark, billowing smoke wrapped around the nightmare, and from within it, the tormented faces of victims briefly appeared as if fighting for release before they were enveloped by the darkness. Before, the throne was a single lone tomb without marking or dedication, a broken stone casket wrapped in iron bars that had been bent outwards. It was a cage torn open from within.

'At long last, I bid you welcome to my home,' the undead greeted as he rose to stand with arms open wide in salutation.

'Lich,' Jaks whispered, voice trembling.

Wraith knew the horror Jaks spoke of from her teachings with the Guild, the last resort of a sorcerer to sustain existence in the face of death. This undeath, a corpse clinging to life at the damnation of its soul, could only exist by draining the essence of others. Upon the walls it was clear to see all who had fallen victim, the cost of their lives to sustain his. Few lichs had ever been encountered, but those recorded were said to be more powerful and deadly than their living selves as body and mind were corrupted by undeath and the twisted arcane and taken souls that sustained them.

'For centuries I have waited, clinging to unlife, trapped within this cage,' Zarakahn uttered as the green aflame eyes glared at a cracked and broken gem in his skeletal fingers. A ruby. 'It was his might that gave me power enough to escape. Power enough to return. Cracks are appearing again, splinters in this world. His realm, long hidden and trapped, is breaking through. His chaos and darkness spills forth. Soon, all in Centuros will know his name... Axuroth.'

At the mention of that name, Wraith looked at Jaks with warning, but the fiend could only see ahead to the horror of the lich.

'For centuries I have waited for one worthy,' Zarakahn said as the skeletal being looked down upon the intruders. 'Now, you are here.'

'Shade, hand over the relic you possess,' Sir Antonius ordered. 'Release to me my ancestral blade.'

'The foolish dreams of men.' The lich laughed. 'Lock-wood, you sacrifice the lives of many for the will and greed of one. Tell me, do you even know why your family was shamed and your home cast to ruin?'

'I care not for past shames.'

'It was the Sacred who purged your home,' Zarakahn said. 'Your family hid one of us, a possessor of arcane. A potential. It is quite the circle of events, do you not agree?

177

Your family cut me down, a sorcerer, and then it was my kind who cast your family down into ruin.' The lich's gaze turned towards Wraith, its green demonic eyes glowing horrifically.

'I care not for your words, abomination,' the knight spat. 'Where is the lance? Where is the blade that ended your miserable life and sentenced you to this undeath?'

'Come and claim it,' Zarakahn taunted, 'if you can.'

The green flames flickered at the lich's last word before the heads upon the bodies on the walls rose and turned towards the crypt's intruders. Wraith and the others recoiled as, from across the floor of the crypt, the skeletal remains of the Lockwood ancestors tremored and rose. Dozens of ancient warriors stood in legion with eye sockets glowing with green flames as they turned to face the living. More rose from other nearby tombs, corpses clawing their way out adorned in aged armour, weapons raised in fury.

'Only death awaits you now,' Zarakahn uttered with cruel delight. 'By my hand, by the fallen, or by the betrayal of those you call friends and allies.'

Suddenly, from behind them, Hammer roared in fury and brought her Warhammer down upon one of Sir Antonius's followers, crushing the skull of the man in a sickening display of gore. The ogre, eyes glowing green and pulsing with foul smoke, then swung her hammer round and struck Badger hard in the chest, sending the gnome druid hurtling across the tomb where she landed, unmoving. Hammer turned on Aederean and Darsil, but Fenrix threw himself in the way, gripping onto the Warhammer and fighting for control.

Petero, one of the Sir Antonius's squires, cried out in agony as the points of two scimitar blades tore through his chest and lifted him high, his murderer Skiminos, who hissed with rage. Like the lich and the ogre, the fiend's eyes glowed horribly green. Skiminos cast down the boy and then sliced his blade across the throat of the nearest man in their company without mercy.

'They have been possessed,' Jaks warned before a crossbow bolt struck her chest just below the shoulder. Quinlan's crossbow bolt. The highborn too looked on in fury with green, smoking eyes as he drew his rapier and turned on Raven. The elf dived away and brought her curved knives up to block his blade, barely able to hold him back.

'Quinlan, stop this!' she pleaded, but the hilt of the rapier punched across her face. Wraith threw herself between them as Quinlan attempted to skewer the elf, Shatter deflecting the falling rapier.

'This is not you,' Wraith called to the highborn. 'Remember yourself. Remember that we are friends.'

Quinlan's reply was a cry of fury as he struck down with his rapier again and again, forcing Wraith back farther towards the waiting skeletons that had surrounded them all. Ducking away, Wraith brought her silver dagger towards the rapier's hilt, impaling a hand and tearing a bloody gash. The rapier fell to the ground, but Quinlan was not diminished, leaping at Wraith and wrapping his hands around her throat. His momentum forced them over and crashing to the ground, Shatter and her silver dagger torn from her grasp by the impact. Unable to breathe, the Slayer kicked and punched Quinlan, but his grip would not lessen. Stars appeared before her eyes until a pale blue hand suddenly reached out and pressed against Quinlan's forehead.

'Rest,' Jaks' voice commanded, and instantly the highborn's eyes closed and he fell unconscious.

Wraith gasped for breath as she pushed Quinlan off her,

the highborn rolling onto the stone floor, head hitting the ground a little too hard.

'Did you… kill him?' Wraith gasped.

'Just asleep,' Jaks replied as she helped Wraith to stand and then pulled the bolt free of her chest with a gasp of pain.

Raven recovered herself and joined them as they looked on at the chaos before them. Fenrix continued to grapple with Hammer, the weyre fighting a losing battle against the larger and stronger ogre as she forced him back and crashing into the far wall. Aederan and Darsil were facing Skimonos as the fiend's deadly scimitars twirled through the air. The dwarf had peppered the fiend with arrows, but he did not stop until Aederan finally managed to flank his foe. With ease, the assassin brutally stabbed Skiminos's side to pierce the heart within. Still the fiend attacked, eyes aglow, until Darsil brought a mace crashing against his skull.

The rest of the survivors looked on in horror as the skeleton masses marched slowly towards them from all sides, though none yet attacked.

'I do not fear the undead,' Sir Antonius roared as he charged forward towards the lich with broadsword held ready.

'You will fear me!' Zarakahn declared as he reached out for the knight and took hold of his armour. The lich pulled the Lockwood descendant close so that his glowing eyes glared into the knight's. Sir Antonius fought for release and to bring his sword to bear, but the lich's arcane gaze stilled his movements. Horror overwhelmed the knight, his mouth open, aghast, and his lips trembling as tears streamed from his eyes.

'Your ancestor cut me down and trapped me in the darkness,' the lich uttered. 'You will forever remember the fear I have instilled in you and the cowardice that now overwhelms you.'

Sir Antonius screamed with horror as the lich's gaze intensified, a spell taking hold and the knight's strength of will broken. Piss soaked his breeches as he was released and immediately crumpled to the ground.

'Now do you fear me?' The lich laughed as it stood over the terrified knight.

Sir Antonius could not manage a single word in reply as he threw his broadsword away and fled, running for the staircase. The knight barged aside two of his followers, forcing one onto the waiting spear of a risen skeleton, and then hurtled up the stone stairs and away, his screams echoing from above.

'The Lockwood cowardice runs deep,' Zarakahn leered.

In reply, Raven loosed an arrow, the shaft soaring across the cavern and striking true, impaling through the lich's left eye.

'You will have to try a lot harder than that,' the undead sorcerer mocked as he pulled the arrow free with ease and let it fall harmlessly to the floor. 'Now, my immortal congregation, bring the chosen to me.'

At the lich's command, the Lockwood dead finally advanced and attacked, eyes aglow with hellish green flames. From all sides they loomed, rusted, aged weaponry still deadly, and empty hands clawing at the intruders who stood in a protective circle around the fallen Quinlan. Wraith cut one down with Shatter but was forced back by an axe that swung in a wide, clumsy arc. The skeleton snarled as smoke streamed from its green eyes before Raven's curved blades tore into its skull. Jaks forced back a handful of the corpses with spear and razor-sharp wings, but the skeletons did not fear the fiend and two of their ancient blades tore across her wings. A claw gripped

Wraith hard upon the shoulder, another tearing across her face as she fought for freedom. Every skeletal warrior they destroyed was replaced by two or three more. Risking a glance across the cavern, Wraith saw that Fenrix was still locked in a losing battle against Hammer, as Aederan, Darsil, and the last of Sir Antonius's men were fighting for survival.

One man broke free of the masses of skeletons and charged the lich, roaring a battle-cry. Zarakahn saw the threat and acted quickly, reaching out and unleashing a pair of fanged bone claws like undead snakes. The claws wrapped around the man, sending him tumbling over and screaming in agony as they ripped him to shreds.

Shatter ripped through the chest of one skeleton but became stuck in its ribcage. The corpse's jaw hung loose, as if laughing in mockery as a spider crawled free of its skull. Wraith began to panic as the undead encircled them with her weapon trapped. Around the Slayer, her allies fought for survival. Bone chains reached out for Jaks, the fiend evading them for a time until they seized her leg and wrist. Eyes aglow, she froze the chains and shattered them with her spear before a score of skeletons stumbled towards her. Quinlan was still out cold, and Raven was struggling to protect him, her quiver now empty and curved knives barely holding back the undead. Fenrix howled with anger as he still fought Hammer, biting and tearing at the ogre, but she would not release him, slamming the weyre into the stone walls with sickening impacts.

Wraith knew they were losing, outnumbered and over-whelmed. Death would claim them soon and they would all be trapped within the Lockwood halls of the dead, at the lich's command. The aches rose within her hands, and though fearful of discovery, she was more fearful of death. Then she remembered the Alchemist's gift. Tearing herself free of the walking corpses, she ducked down and rifled through the pockets of her cloak. Wraith pulled free the vial containing a milky white fluid with shimmering flakes.

'Only when you have no other choice,' Wraith repeated before tearing the cork free with her teeth, spitting it away and then downing the vial's contents in one gulp.

She felt the potion's effects instantly, a different fire burning within. It stretched out across her body, gifting her an energy she had never possessed. Around her, the skeletons, her friends and allies, even Zarakahn, all began to slow, but Wraith realised it was actually that she was moving faster than any of them. The potion had gifted her speed and agility, and she must use it to save those around her. She rose, and taking hold of the hilt of her trapped shortsword, kicked the skeleton hard in chest, freeing her blade.

With Shatter in one hand and a recovered ancient shield in the other, she tore through the corpses surrounding herself, Raven, and Jaks. She evaded their slow and cumbersome swings and rammed the shield into their skeletal forms, knocking them back and shattering them on the stone walls and ground. The Slayer released her shortsword and drew two throwing daggers, launching them towards Hammer to impale in the ogre's back. She then caught Shatter before the blade could hit the ground. The ogre recoiled at the pain, gifting Fenrix a moment to strike and bring his axe up and into his foe's chest.

Wraith then turned on the lich. Already she could feel the potion's effects begin to wane, and she sprinted towards Zarakahn, shield held high and Shatter ready to deliver the killing blow. Green energy surged towards her from the lich's outstretched hand, the shield taking the brunt of the impact. She ran on, and when close enough, rammed Shatter into the lich's chest.

The green aflame eyes of Zarakahn stared into Wraith's before a deep, terrible laughter emanated from him. The shortsword had not fazed the lich, and his skeletal hand took hold of Wraith's armour and lifted her from her feet. Shatter and the shield were torn from her grasp, and the Slayer was held helpless over the undead sorcerer. Terrified, she looked down upon its ruined body and saw that the blade and hilt of a broken sword was impaled in the lich's back.

'I offered you everything,' Zarakahn sneered. 'Now I will take it from you. You possess all I need, my dear girl. You will be my vessel, and with it, I shall escape this prison.'

I cannot let this evil escape to the world, Wraith realised, and she reached into herself, drawing upon that ache that always lingered and threatened to escape.

'NOO!' Wraith screamed as the hidden fire within her rose and surged free, flames leaping from her palms to engulf the skeletal lich.

Despite the roaring flames, the lich's grip did not lessen.

'You possess all I need,' Zarakahn repeated as he reached up with his free hand towards her.

Green energy surged from the lich's fingers and wrapped around Wraith as waves of sickening dread coursed through her. It was terrible, the feeling as if part of her life, her very soul, was being ripped from her and replaced by a chilling cold.

A roar sounded, and Wraith was released and dropped to the ground. She tumbled, rolling clear, and looked back to the throne of bones and the lich. He stood against her friends, Fenrix, Raven, and Jaks. They attacked with axe, knives, and spear, the lich simply standing there and welcoming the assault. Around them, the skeletons amassed again, awaiting their master's orders.

'Your pathetic efforts, whilst amusing, only serve to delay the inevitable.' Zarakahn laughed.

The potion's effects were gone, leaving Wraith aching and exhausted, but she knew she had to re-join the fight. She drew her last remaining weapon, her silver Guild dagger, and readied herself for one last charge.

'Alena...' a weak voice called from the wall near to where Wraith landed.

Upon the walls were the husks and skeletal remains of dozens of victims of all races. Only one still had life to him, but he looked nothing like the boy Wraith had once known. His flesh was grey and withered, barely clinging to the bones beneath. The eyes, once blue, were now shining green. The hair, once blond and fair, was now white and withered. He was held by chains forged of bones, fusing the victim to the wall.

'Luthor...' Wraith stammered as she pulled herself up and towards him. 'I have to get you out. I have to get you free.'

'You can't...' he said, pained by his every word and breath. 'You have to...'

Zarakahn let out a shriek as he reached towards his captive, flickering green light joining them and drawing screams from Luthor. Wraith was forced back by the blast, the light the same terrible deathly energy that had tried to overwhelm her. Instead, it drained the life from Luthor, aging him before Wraith's eyes until the link was broken. The lich, infused with energy, released it in a terrible blast of undead arcane that threw Fenrix, Raven, and Jaks hurtling back. Zarakahn was not finished, his vile laughter returning as his eyes glowed and he uttered the word 'RISE.'

The ruined bodies of Badger, Hammer, Skiminos, and all the others who had perished within the crypt tremored and rose, undead returning to the lich's cause. Zarakahn stepped down and approached Jaks, a smile growing across his withered face.

'A young, fiendish sorcerer,' he jeered. 'The boy was not enough. None of them were, but I sense great potential in you. You possess what I need, and you will gift me release from this hell.'

Zarakahn reached down and emitted the deathly wave of energy upon Jaks, the fiend screaming in terrible agony.

'Alena...' Luthor called to her weakly. 'Alena... please. You know what you have to do.'

His eyes fell upon the silver dagger in Wraith's hand.

'Please...' he said. 'Release me... and cast him back to the... to the afterlife.'

'No, I can't,' Wraith cried. 'I only just found you.'

'I knew... I knew you would,' Luthor said, with tears in his eyes. 'Thank you for always... for always finding me... but you must do this.'

Jaks's screams grew more terrible as she fought a losing battle against the lich's undead strength. Fenrix, Raven, and all the others struggled for survival against the vast numbers of newly risen corpses.

'Alena... you must do this now...' Luthor pleaded. 'End him... by freeing me.'

Wraith lifted her dagger towards him, tears falling from her eyes before stopping and placing a hand to his cheek in comfort.

'NO!' Zarakahn screamed as he realised the danger all too late. 'NO! GET AWAY FROM HIM!'

'Thank you,' Wraith told Luthor, 'for being a friend to me when I had no one.'

He smiled and then closed his eyes as Wraith closed

hers. The silver dagger found his heart, ending his life, as was his wish.

Zarakahn howled a terrible scream as green smoke emanated from his entire undead body as he trembled and shook, falling to his knees. The lich reached towards Jaks and all those still living, seeking desperately to use them as he had Luthor to survive. A feeble green light stretched from the lich's withered fingers, but a shield blocked its path, wielded by the recovered Quinlan. The highborn held firm and drove back the lich's arcane as the undead sorcerer let out one final, terrible scream. The legion of skeletal warriors and risen dead collapsed and fell still once again before a green flicker of light erupted from Zarakahn's chest. His already withered body crumbled and faded, falling as dust amongst its ruined robes and the clatter of a sword falling to the ground echoed throughout the chamber.

Quinlan was the first to act, running forward and recovering the broken blade, the Lockwood Lance, from the lich's remains, as well as the cracked and ruined ruby. The highborn held the relic high in triumph, cheering aloud before realising that Fenrix, Raven, and Jaks were glaring at him.

'What?' he asked innocently. 'Wait… did I shoot you, Jaks? And when did I cut my hand open?'

Wraith turned away from them, and with tears still in her eyes and on her cheeks, she recovered Shatter and turned back to Luthor. Though her body cried out from the punishment it had suffered and demanded rest, she lifted her weary arm and hacked at the bone chains holding Luthor. She grunted with the effort, angry tears escaping as she struck again and again.

'Wraith, wait,' Raven called to her in sympathy and support. 'You can barely stand.'

'I don't care,' Wraith spat back. 'I cannot leave him here.'

Quinlan bandaged the hand that was cut by Wraith and came to her aid, alongside Raven. Though equally weary and suffering, they silently helped in cutting Luthor free and gently lowered his body to the ground. Fenrix lifted the body of Badger in his arms, letting out a long howl of mourning. Jaks stood over the remains of the lich and spat on the dust.

'I hope you rot in whatever afterlife has claimed you,' the fiend swore. 'Rot and burn.'

CHAPTER SEVENTEEN
THE RUINED FORTRESS OF KARNOCK

Over thirty people entered the Lockwood Mausoleum over the past two days. Now, a mere eight emerged; Wraith and her allies, Aederan, Darsil, and Mason. When the undead lich began his attack, Aederan forced the boy into an empty stone casket to hide. He was fortunate, but many others were not so lucky. With what oil and wood they could scavenge, the tomb was set to flames, the bodies of Hammer, Skiminos, and so many others among them. Only two were carried out, both on the shoulders of Fenrix; Badger, who had shown him such care, and Luthor, the lost Guild apprentice. Neither Wraith nor Fenrix wanted to leave them down there, and so, despite the wounds and sheer exhaustion, the weyre carried them both as he uttered prayers to Daegon, God of death and the afterlife.

'We should bury her in the woods nearby.' Fenrix looked at the gnome in his arms. Her eyes were closed, as if she was merely sleeping.

'She would have liked that,' Aederan said, as Darsil

wiped tears from his eyes. 'Returned to the nature she loved so much.'

'She deserved better for all the kindness she showed us,' the dwarf said, heartbroken.

'What of your friend?' Raven asked Wraith.

'To the woods too,' the Slayer said. 'At least with Badger, he will have company. He never did like being alone.'

'Are you going to be all right?' Raven asked, but Wraith ignored the concern.

'Did anyone see?' she asked back in a whisper.

'The lich set himself ablaze as he held you up high,' the elf replied quietly. 'No one saw. We were all too busy fighting for survival… or unconscious, in Quinlan's case.'

'Thank you,' Wraith said softly.

'We lay our lost friends to rest and then rest ourselves,' Jaks said wearily. 'I could sleep for a week.'

'Here, you should have this,' Quinlan said as he handed the Lockwood Lance over to Wraith.

The Slayer held the blade to the light. It was just as the viscount had described it; a broken blade tainted black by blood, a sapphire gem at the centre of the cross-guard, and a jade stone at the pommel. Many lives had been lost for that ruined weapon, that relic of a time long ago.

Wraith smelt his foul stench of piss and shit and vomit before she felt the edge of his blade against her neck. Instinctively, she lifted the lance away and out of his reach.

'You will hand that to me,' Sir Antonius Lockwood ordered, the knight wide-eyed and trembling.

'Sir Lockwood, don't do this,' Aederan implored as all turned to face the knight as he held a sword to Wraith's throat. Fenrix growled menacingly, Raven edged closer with knife in hand, Jaks readied her spear, and Quinlan…

'C'mon!' the highborn shouted to the sky above. 'This is

over! We dragged ourselves through hell down there and now this!'

'You and the dwarf are still under my employ,' the knight said through gritted teeth to Aederan. 'Stand with me now or you forgo your payment. See the blade into my hand.'

'You do not want to go down this path,' Wraith said calmly to her captor.

'Hand over the Lockwood Lance, or I will be forced to end your life,' Sir Antonius replied as he applied pressure on his sword and drew a trickle of blood down Wraith's neck.

'Do you think my companions will just let you leave here with it?' the Slayer asked.

'I cannot leave empty-handed,' the knight cried, his resolve already broken by the lich's curse. 'I have nothing! No title, no lands, and no gold but what little I carried with me. I am ruined if I do not succeed here.'

'What about our pay?' Darsil yelled angrily.

'Only with the Lockwood fortune, which will be mine once I have the Lance,' Sir Antonius promised, though his words did little to convince them.

'Now all oppose you,' Wraith said. 'Release me and you can still leave here with your life.'

'It is too late for that,' Sir Antonius said manically. 'I am disgraced and shamed. If I cannot have the lance, then neither can you.'

The knight screamed and reached back, swinging his broadsword towards Wraith's neck, but he stopped just before the blade could touch her flesh. Sir Antonius arched his back, spluttering blood from his lips as he turned and revealed a spear buried deep in his side.

'Mason...' the knight muttered as he saw it was the squire who delivered the blow. Sir Antonius stumbled to his knees and then collapsed to the ground, hand still reaching for the Lockwood Lance as death took him.

'For all who lost their lives in your foolish crusade,' Mason spat.

'Thank you,' Wraith said to the squire as she wiped the blood from her throat.

'Where will I go now?' Mason asked as he looked down on his fallen master. 'I've no family or home but with him.'

'You can stay with us, lad,' Aederan offered. 'We will see you to the nearest town, or seeing as how deadly you are with a spear, you might want to stay with us a while longer.'

The boy merely nodded his thanks.

'What now?' Wraith asked Aederan as she secured the remains of the Lockwood Lance within her cloak. 'No bloodshed within the Guild, but outside is a different story. Those are our rules, are they not? Will you try to take the lance next?'

'Perhaps I should.' The assassin grinned, drawing a nervous look from Wraith's companions. 'After all, none of you look in well enough state for another fight. Thanks to that fool's lies I am out of pocket and have seen half of my group lost to the evil of this mausoleum.'

'Just say the word, boss.' Darsil laughed merrily with an arrow notched upon his bow, but unraised.

Aederan paused for a moment, but then his warm smile returned. 'No.' the elf said. 'The contract and its rewards are yours. If it were not for you and your group, I do not think any of us would have escaped those crypts, and that lich would have escaped to the surface and cast his damnation upon us all. You have my thanks this day, but it might not always be so.'

'Empty-handed again,' his dwarven companion muttered.

'I'm sure we can sell on some of the knight's gaudy possessions,' Aederan said. 'And don't forget the pelts of the wolves who attacked us. They will fetch a fine penny or two, not to mention the gold and gems taken from the crypts that now fill our pockets.'

'It was an honour working with you,' Wraith said with a hand offered.

'If you are ever in our dear capital city of Aelthorn, I do hope you and your friends will seek us out,' Aederan said as he took Wraith's hand and gripped tight.

'Do not think I have forgotten our bet,' Quinlan called after Darsil. 'Two hundred gold coins.'

'What makes you think I have that on me.' The dwarf laughed before he tossed Luthor's silver dagger to them. 'Keep it. Until next time, Forsaken.'

'Next time.' Quinlan chuckled as he handed the dagger to Wraith.

'Enough talk,' Aederan said. 'We bury our dead, pay our respects, and share a drink in their honour.'

'Then we get the hell out of this place,' Raven said.

'To Rheins to rid ourselves of that cursed lance and then on to home,' Jaks said to Wraith.

'Home,' the Slayer agreed as she looked from the silver dagger to the frail body of Luthor. The home she had with the Guild would never be the same without him, but the word *home* also reminded her of another, a place of family amongst the snow.

CHAPTER EIGHTEEN
LOCKWOOD ESTATE

THE CITY OF RHEINS

'I can scarcely believe my eyes,' Viscount Christoph Lockwood applauded in his cold and calculating tone as he took hold of the Lockwood Lance and lifted it high. 'Never in my wildest delusions could I have believed that you, out of all of those who have taken the contract, could have completed it. Miracles really can happen.'

'You wanted the blade, and you now have it,' Wraith said, with Raven and Jaks at her side in the viscount's study. Fenrix, again, was not permitted entry, and Quinlan could not be dragged from the nearest inn once they had arrived in the city.

'Now, for our payment?' Wraith asked.

'With this symbol, I will unite the Lockwood family under my command,' the viscount said with narrowed eyes and dreams of glory, lost in his own victory. 'United, I will see to it that we are purged of the weak and spineless who have cast us into the dirt. The Lockwood name will rise to distinction once again as a ruling house of Castille. Even those in the capital, King Rothgard among them, will acknowledge our prominence.'

'Our payment?' Wraith repeated, but still their employer did not respond.

Jaks, growing impatient, slammed the butt of her staff upon the floor. A deep, resonating boom sounded from the impact, shaking the study and finally snapping the viscount from his daze.

'We have come too far and endured too much to be ignored now,' the fiend said.

'And you do not know what it cost us,' Wraith added with a hand upon Luthor's dagger beneath her cloak.

'Payment, yes,' the viscount said, unfazed by the sorcerer's flare of anger and arcane. He slowly crossed the office, and from his papers, lifted a single piece of parchment.

'I have waited a long time for this to be claimed,' he said, blowing dust from the page as he handed it over. 'Give that to my clerk downstairs. She will see to it that you receive your reward.'

'And this will be proof that the contract was fulfilled,' Wraith said as she took the parchment and saw that it was signed with the Lockwood seal and coat of arms.

'I must remember the name of your resourceful little band,' the viscount said as his gaze returned to the lance. 'I am certain that I will have use for you in the near future. Now, our business is complete. Retrieve your payment and leave my presence.'

'Gladly,' Wraith said, with parchment held tight.

Escorted by the Lockwood guards, Wraith, Raven, and Jaks were led back downstairs and to the entrance of the estate. There, they waited whilst the clerk was summoned, and upon seeing the parchment, ordered the reward to be gathered from the vault.

'So, the rumour is true,' called the shrill, taunting voice

of Lady Aureilia Lockwood as she approached. 'The Lockwood Lance has been retrieved, and by the most unlikely of all those who took on the challenge. What is most shocking is that you accomplished the task with your very apparent disadvantage.'

The elven noblewoman looked to Raven, the *disadvantage* she saw in their group, and grimaced.

'Lady Lockwood,' Wraith greeted through clenched teeth as she forced herself to bow before the noble. Raven did the same, as did Jaks, the sorcerer masking her identity for the moment. No member of the order of the Sacred need bow to noble or royalty.

'Tell me, did you succeed in my task also?' Lady Lockwood asked.

'Unfortunately, the tombs had already been looted by many,' Wraith explained. 'All but the most guarded of crypts were looted a dozen times over.

'And those that were most guarded?' Lady Lockwood asked. 'Tell me, what did they possess?'

'Horror unimaginable,' Jaks said, the fiend leaning in close, eyes alive with arcane might.

Lady Lockwood was taken aback by a moment, confused before all were disturbed by the arrival of guards carrying five small chests.

'And here is your reward,' Lady Lockwood said dismissively. 'A fortune to you, I am certain, but a paltry insignificance for us. Try not to waste it too soon or I am sure you will return to the gutter whence you came.'

Those last words were directed solely at Raven, the elven noblewoman still baring a strong dislike for the former-slave. Raven did not reply, words lost. She could only turn away in shame.

'Oh, how foolish of me,' Wraith suddenly said as she turned to Jaks and rummaged through the fiend's pouches.

The sorcerer was about to question and push away the Slayer before realising her intent. Raven too realised late and could only look on in shock.

'There was one item of worth we thought you would be interested in,' Wraith said as she produced from a tightly bound piece of cloth a simple golden circlet. Wraith made certain to only touch the item by the cloth that held it.

'It was found in the most sacred of Lockwood tombs,' Jaks added with a sudden pompous, highborn accent, 'belonging to a lady of the family with some high reputation by the extravagant tomb that had been erected in her honour. Sadly, the lady's name was lost to time, but the circlet remains.'

'It is a simple band of gold,' Lady Lockwood said with indifference, 'but I will take it, nonetheless. Will ten gold suffice?'

'It is more than enough, milady.' Wraith bowed as she covered the circlet in the cloth again and handed it over.

'Will you fine gentlemen please escort these chests outside with us,' Jaks asked with her ridiculous noble voice. 'A companion awaits who will be able to carry them.'

'Make quick work of it,' Lady Lockwood ordered as she pulled the cloth away so she could inspect her newly purchased circlet closer.

Wraith, Raven, and Jaks quickly escaped the estate, meeting Fenrix outside, who took two of the chests from the nervous guardsmen as the others took one each. The guards waited for some form of payment for their small duty but were quickly scared away by the sudden howl of the weyre. The roar was quickly followed by a scream of terror from within the estate that could only have been from Lady Lockwood.

'Trouble again?' Fenrix asked, though he already knew the answer.

'I think it best we leave this city,' Wraith said as she urged them away down the street.

'Thank you,' Raven said to the Slayer as they all quickened their pace. 'You did not need to do that.'

'Yes, I did,' Wraith replied with a smile of certainty.

'If she hadn't, I would have,' Jaks agreed. 'Besides, they will never dare attempt to retaliate against a member of the Sacred.'

'Nobody speaks down to our friends like that,' Wraith said. 'We may be Forsaken, but we have each other.'

'She's lucky I didn't turn her into a toad.' Jaks laughed.

'You can do that?' Raven questioned.

'Where do you think our friend Quinlan really is?' the fiend asked with a wink and a pat on her pocket. 'I owed him for the crossbow bolt he shot me with!'

'Wait, wait!' a voice yelled from the street as a man ran towards them. 'Please, wait!'

The group turned to see it was none other than Jefford Hencaster, flustered, red-faced, wide-eyed, and panting as he came to a sudden stop before them.

'Thank the Gods... I found you!' he gasped as he leant over and breathed hard. 'I heard of your return... and feared you had already... left us.'

'We were just leaving,' Raven said.

'Steady yourself,' Wraith urged the merchant. 'What's wrong?'

'I have need of you,' Jefford said as he straightened up and looked at the Slayer with a hardened gaze. 'I have a contract... an urgent contract for you.'

'We just finished one contract,' Fenrix growled.

'And were headed home,' Raven warned.

'For rest and sleep,' Jaks added. 'Days of sleep.'

'I need you. All of you. Now,' Jefford swore. 'I will pay

for your services... but we must act now. A great many lives are at stake, and we need a Slayer!'

'We really shouldn't linger here,' Raven warned with a glance back towards the Lockwood Estate.

Wraith looked from her allies, battered, bruised, and exhausted, and then to the urgency of the merchant. Beyond them, voices could be heard calling out in several directions, cries of warning, panic, and a monster risen from the waves. The people were fleeing the streets, running and seeking what shelter they could.

'We need you,' Jefford pleaded.

Wraith looked to Raven, Fenrix, and Jaks, and found all of them looking straight back with readiness in their eyes. They had already followed her into one nightmare and were prepared to do so again. Raven nodded to Wraith as she drew her curved knives. Fenrix howled as he lifted his axe high to greet the coming fight. Jaks's eyes flickered with arcane as a smile crept across her lips. From her pocket, she pulled forth a green, slimy toad.

'Better turn Quinlan back,' Wraith said to the sorcerer with a wink before turning to Jefford Hencaster.

'The Forsaken will answer the call,' Wraith vowed with her hand upon her arrowhead necklace. 'Now, show us this beastie.'

EPILOGUE
SKYPEAK MOUNTAINS

In the midst of a terrible blizzard upon the mountain, a lone dwarf dug at the snow-covered ground with bare hands. His fingers would have blackened with frostbite, but the flesh and nails were torn away by his efforts, bone scraping amongst the dirt. Though the pain had to be excruciating, the dwarf showed no recognition, his focus only on his goal. An amulet hung loose from around his neck, its ruby glowing bright amidst the snowstorm.

Deeper. Deeper. The voice called to Blain Ironhill. *Do not stop when we are so close.*

The dwarf continued his efforts, undaunted by the pain, the cold, and the storm around him. His hair and thick beard were frozen solid, skin black and blue where the frost had killed the flesh. He dug deeper and deeper, ruined hands clawing through the earth until finally something was discovered. From amongst the dirt, he uncovered bodily remains, rot, bones, and rags buried deep upon the mountain.

My patron's final resting place, the voice said. It was not sorrow in its tone, but eager anticipation.

From amidst the remains was one piece that showed no decay nor ruin or flaw; a single crimson ruby near identical to that on the amulet around Blain's neck. When lifted into the dwarf's hand, the gem flickered and shone, and Blain's amulet matched its pulsation like a heartbeat.

Well done, my friend, the voice encouraged. *You have come further than many before you. Our journey together continues, and the realms will soon remember us.*

'Yes... Axuroth...' Blain smiled as he rose up to stand, turned south, and began pacing down the mountainside.

WRAITH AND HER ALLIES WILL RETURN IN

THE FORSAKEN: CARNEVIL